THE GOOD DIE YOUNG

DI SALLY PARKER
BOOK ELEVEN

M A COMLEY

For my rock, my beautiful mother, who is now watching over me. Dementia sucks. Remembering all the good times we shared together.

You took a huge chunk of my heart with you. Love you and will miss you, until we're reunited once more.

ACKNOWLEDGMENTS

Special thanks as always go to @studioenp for their superb cover design expertise.

My heartfelt thanks go to my wonderful editor Emmy and my proofreaders Joseph and Barbara for spotting all the lingering nits.

Thank you also to my amazing ARC Group who help to keep me sane during this process.

To Mary, gone, but never forgotten. I hope you found the peace you were searching for my dear friend. I miss you each and every day.

ALSO BY M A COMLEY

The Kill List (DI Sara Ramsey #15)

Crossing The Line (DI Sara Ramsey #16)

Time to Kill (DI Sara Ramsey #17)

Deadly Passion (DI Sara Ramsey #18)

Son of the Dead (DI Sara Ramsey#19)

Evil Intent (DI Sara Ramsey #20)

The Games People Play (DI Sara Ramsey #21)

Revenge Streak (DI Sara Ramsey #22)

I Know The Truth (A Psychological thriller)

She's Gone (A psychological thriller)

Shattered Lives (A psychological thriller)

Evil In Disguise – a novel based on True events

Deadly Act (Hero series novella)

Torn Apart (Hero series #1)

End Result (Hero series #2)

In Plain Sight (Hero Series #3)

Double Jeopardy (Hero Series #4)

Criminal Actions (Hero Series #5)

Regrets Mean Nothing (Hero series #6)

Prowlers (Di Hero Series #7)

Sole Intention (Intention series #1)

Grave Intention (Intention series #2)

Devious Intention (Intention #3)

Cozy mysteries

Murder at the Wedding

Murder at the Hotel

Murder by the Sea

Death on the Coast

Death By Association

Merry Widow (A Lorne Simpkins short story)

It's A Dog's Life (A Lorne Simpkins short story)

A Time To Heal (A Sweet Romance)

A Time For Change (A Sweet Romance)

High Spirits

The Temptation series (Romantic Suspense/New Adult Novellas)

Past Temptation

Lost Temptation

Clever Deception (co-written by Linda S Prather)

Tragic Deception (co-written by Linda S Prather)

Sinful Deception (co-written by Linda S Prather)

PROLOGUE

here were some days Timothy Farrant was determined to make his dreams come true, and others he could just take off somewhere and never come back. The latter was definitely an option he was considering today. The amount of work vying for his attention on his desk was mind-boggling. If only the phone would stop ringing long enough for him to tackle his daily chore without interruption, that would indeed be an absolute bonus to his working day.

He'd put in over a hundred hours already this week, barely seen his family, sleeping at the office a few nights, only managing to grab a couple of hours each night before he wiped the sleep out of his eyes and got back in his chair behind his austere executive desk. Up until the last couple of months, he'd regarded his work as take it or leave it, mainly because his partner had taken on the brunt of the office work, while he dealt with the factory side of things, down there on the production floor. That had all changed when Matthew had announced he was selling his stake in the company and taking off, leaving the UK to travel the world while he was still young enough to appreciate what it had to offer.

Timothy had stood there, gaping. Astounded by the revelation, especially as the business had turned a corner in the past few years and was producing more than double it had put out in the last two years alone. "You what?"

"You heard me. I'm not in the habit of repeating myself. I want to get out there while I'm still able to walk and explore every orifice this world has to offer. What's the point of living, if all we do is work our bollocks off around here twelve, fourteen, or even more hours a damn day? It's not like we're reaping the rewards, is it?"

"Christ almighty, that's a warped way of looking at things. To me, that means it's an ideal time for us to put our heads together and come up with a few new ideas to get us out of the rut we're in. But no, not you, you'd rather throw in the towel and jump fucking ship! Give me bloody strength."

"It is what it is. The decision has been made, and it's not up for debate. I leave at the end of this week."

Tim had stared at him for what seemed an age, his mind whirling for a split second, thinking of all the unimaginable ways he could do harm to his partner. "But you can't, not yet, not when we have unfinished business to deal with, I won't allow it."

Matthew had laughed. "You *won't* allow it? Like you have a say in my decision one way or the other. The deal has been done. Done and dusted. Signed on the dotted line. Am I making myself clear now?"

Tim had sunk into the chair next to him, and he'd placed his head in his hands. Finally, after a lot of soul searching, he'd glanced up and asked, "What deal? Who with?"

"You'll find out soon enough, mate, believe me. Now, if you'll excuse me, I must begin clearing out my office."

"As in you're leaving?"

"Jesus, you need to wash your ears out now and again. I said I was leaving at the end of tomorrow, but from this day forward, every aspect of running the factory will fall on your shoulders—that is until the new owner walks through the front door."

"Fuck, man. I demand to know who you've sold your share of the company to. You owe me that much after working alongside you for the past ten years or more. Shit, how did it come to this?"

"How indeed. It's not like I haven't been saying how dissatisfied I am with the way the business was heading over the last few months, is it? Like I've already stated, you need to wash out those ears of yours occasionally and really listen to what's being said to you. Go on, give it a shot, it's surprising what you'll learn. There you go, put that down to vital information that I provided you with before I hit the road to destinations unknown."

"You're a first-class wanker if you think you can get away with this, Matthew."

"*Think* I can get away with it? I've got news for you, part-ner, I *have* got away with it. The funds will be in my bank account by the end of the day. Out of courtesy and because I'm that kind of guy, I've told the new partner that I will continue to guide the ship until Friday, at five, and then I'm out of here, riding off into the sunset to pastures new."

"Screw you, arsehole. Come on, what are the terms of the deal you've struck with this mystery buyer? I have a legal right to know what's been set up behind my back, and I'm warning you, I'll fight it all the way through the courts if necessary."

"I think you'll find your solicitor knows all about it. He's been trying to contact you all week. Word has it that you've been too busy to get back to him."

The truth had hit Tim in the solar plexus like an Exocet

missile. It was true, Arnold had left several urgent messages on his phone, and Tim had delayed responding, only thinking about it once the solicitor had gone home, because unlike Tim, Arnold had a life and was able to switch off at the end of the working day. Tim had stormed out of Matthew's office and rung Arnold right away.

"At last, nice of you to get back to me. I have news for you, Tim, you're not the only client I have who is flat out, day in and day out. The problem is, the others know that when I call it's usually concerning something that is worth listening to. Shame you can't do the bloody same. Still, it's too late for all that now."

"Meaning?"

"What? And still, I don't get an apology from you? You've sunk to a new level, even for you."

"I'm sorry," Tim had muttered the reluctant apology. "Just tell me what the fuck has been going on."

"I'm sure you're aware by now that Matthew has sold his share in the company."

"I've just heard, how? How does that frigging happen without me having a say in the matter?"

"You need to read the small print in your contract. It clearly states that if a buyer comes along and offers either party double what they invested in the company, either party can sell up with just a week's notice. Matthew took up that option. And here we stand."

"Up shit creek, some might say, including me. How has it come to this? Why haven't you had my back on this one, Arnold?"

"You have the audacity to blame me for your cockups? You've got a nerve, Tim. According to Matthew, things haven't been right between you for some time. To normal people involved with a dissatisfied partner, this situation wouldn't come as a surprise to them. I've tried contacting you all week, and you haven't had either the decency or courtesy to get back to me until now. What does that tell you, Tim?"

"That I've been up to my eyes in work. Ever heard of emailing your client if they don't get back to you?"

"Get real. I've sent several urgent emails to you during the week, as well."

Tim had sat at his desk and checked his email account. Nope, there had been nothing sitting in his inbox. He'd bitten down on his tongue until he'd flicked over to the junk mail tab and, bingo, there they were, ten emails or more from Arnold Yates, his solicitor. "Crap, it would appear that I owe you an apology. All your emails are sitting in my junk folder. How that happened, I don't know. Blasted technology has gone to pot lately."

"I'm glad you've been able to confirm that I'm not going round the twist. I had my doubts there for a moment or two."

"No, it's me who is going nuts. I know I've taken my eye off the ball around here lately but I've been dealing with this new product range we're getting ready to launch, and everything else has been put on the back-burner, as it were."

"Which is why your new partner was interested in doing the deal."

"Oh right, and pray, are you going to share the details of this new partner with me?"

"It's all in my first email. Read that and get back to me if you have any further questions on the topic. I've got to go, I have another client waiting to see me." With that, his solicitor had hung up.

"What the fuck? Am I invisible all of a sudden, or what? Don't I matter any more, despite owning fifty percent of this effing company?" He'd swallowed down his pride, grabbed a coffee from the machine that was permanently on the go in the corner of the room and put his reading glasses on to scan over Arnold's first email.

Instead of feeling bitter and angry, he'd chilled to a new level after consuming the contents. Everything, on paper at least, seemed to be okay in his eyes. The new owner was a woman, Barbara Cotton, who was determined to continue as a silent partner in the business, especially when everything appeared to be going according to plan with regard to the development and growth of the company.

He'd sat back, sipped at his drink and read through the other emails Arnold had sent him. An overwhelming sense of shame had suddenly descended, so much so that he bucked up his ideas and left his office. He'd tapped on Matthew's door and stuck his head around it when he'd been beckoned a few seconds later.

"Umm... I think I owe you an apology, pal."

"And some. This was all done for the good of the business, Tim. You're far more involved in this than I am. The last six months, doing everything needed to get this new product range to the market has absolutely drained me. My homelife has suffered to the extent that Sandra threatened to walk out on me if things didn't change. You know what that would do to me, I've loved that girl since our first day at university. I couldn't allow that to happen. I didn't do this out of spite, I've done it out of necessity to save the company, my marriage and my sanity, all bundled into one neat package. Do your research on this woman, she's been amazing over the past decade in this trade. Taking several companies that were on the brink of collapse and turning them around, transforming them into multi-million-pound investments."

"That may be so, then what? She sells them on for a huge profit?"

"You'll have to ask her that. I don't think so, but I think possibly the odd one here and there along the way when she felt the need to sell on. Who knows what the reasons are behind that?"

"I guess she and I are going to have to spend a whole day discussing this, once she comes in and finally introduces herself."

Matthew had wagged a finger. "Not going to happen. I think you'll find the day-to-day running of the factory is going to fall on your shoulders. She's intending to be a silent partner."

"Fuck, man. Talk about heaping the bloody work on me. What the actual fuck? How can a business this size sustain just me being at the helm? I'm flat out most days, walking the factory floor, while you deal with all the office paperwork and shit, and now, all of a sudden, I'm expected to do it all? It ain't gonna happen, not if we—sorry, I—want this business to thrive in the future. I refuse to kill myself, working all the hours under the sun just to bring profits to the table for a silent partner. What happens if I fail?"

Matthew had shrugged. "You'll have to ask her that, although I can probably guess what her answer will be."

"Go on?"

"No profit means no company. It'll be put back on the market in an instant."

"Christ, and I'm supposed to put up with crap like that?"

"I don't think you've got an option. It's up to you to make the business a success."

"That much is obvious." He'd turned and walked out of his partner's office, a sense of despair clawing at his insides, and returned to his own office where he had finished off reading the emails from his complacent solicitor, at least in his eyes.

· · ·

WEEKS LATER, with the business now in the hands of a silent partner, his life was stretched to the maximum. His marriage was on severely shaky ground, and his kids treated him like a stranger every time he dared to set foot in the house, which wasn't often lately. He was beginning to wonder if Matthew hadn't done the right thing selling up, after all. Ploughing on, he finished up the first pile of paperwork on his to-do list and decided to stretch his legs and walk round the factory floor, to ensure everything was going to plan down there with the new line. He felt blessed, having just taken on a new manager to oversee things in his absence. Gary was a dab hand at keeping the staff on their toes and making sure things ran smoothly on the production line. Tim's stomach clenched every time he wandered past the new machinery. There had been a few hiccups to begin with, but now everything appeared to be running like clockwork for the big day.

"All right, Gary?"

"Yes, boss. We'll be ready to rock and roll on the day. I've made a few tweaks to up the output without stretching the staff to their limits." He lowered his voice and added, "That should raise the production to another level. Maybe get us another twenty boxes an hour more than we anticipated."

Tim winked and patted Gary on the shoulder. "Good man. They'll soon get used to the extra pace, it'll become second nature to them in no time at all."

"Here's hoping. Anything else I can do to ease your stress levels, boss?"

"I can't think of anything right now. Just keep up the good work, and we'll reap the rewards soon enough. Remember there's a huge bonus on the table for you, *if* we can pull this off."

"I'll be counting on that. The missus has already spent it on a new extension to the kitchen."

They both laughed.

"Typical, eh? What are these women like?"

"Yep, I'd be lost without her all the same. She keeps me on the straight and narrow, there's no doubt about it."

Tim continued his rounds and then went outside, needing to feel the wind on his face. "So, this is what fresh air feels like, I'd totally forgotten."

His mobile rang while he was having a sneaky fag. Distracted, he said, "Hello, Tim Farrant."

"Hello, Tim. It's me again."

He froze on the spot and stubbed out his cigarette on the brick wall beside him. His heart racing, he paced the loading bay area, constantly casting a glance over his shoulder. "What... what do you want?"

"Now, now, Timmy boy," the male said in the sing-song tone Tim had grown to hate since the man had first contacted him several weeks before.

"You know exactly what I want. I've given you more than enough breathing time to consider putting your plan into action. Have you done it yet?"

"No, I told you, I'm up to my neck in work and I haven't got any spare time at present."

"Tut-tut. Excuses, excuses. We need to get you back on track. I fear there's only one way we're going to be able to do that."

"No, please don't. I'm not making excuses; I genuinely haven't been home to see my family in days."

"So, you won't have heard then..."

Tim closed his eyes, fearing what the man was about to say. "What?"

There was a long pause on the other end of the line.

"Hello, are you still there?" Tim asked.

"I'm here. Young Cally..."

"No, what about my daughter? What have you done to her?"

"Nothing... yet. But if you keep dragging your feet that will change soon, that's a promise. Do the right thing, Tim. You were warned not to produce the new line. You lied to me. I have it on good authority that everything is on track and the production line is going to be working at full pelt soon enough. Wrong move!" The menacing caller hung up.

Tim slammed against the wall and slid down it to rest on his haunches.

What the fuck? He's got me by the short and curlies and is threatening my family now. I can't... I refuse to put them at risk.

At that moment, the back door flew open. A member of staff walked out, saw him and scampered inside again. He jumped to his feet and followed the young man into the building. The youngster made eye contact with him. Tim wagged his finger and shook his head. The guy had the decency to look embarrassed at being caught out. Tim hopped in the lift and went up to his office to be told by his secretary, Thelma, that Barbara Cotton had been on the phone and had requested a call back.

Shit, so much for her being a silent partner.

After topping up his mug of coffee, he plucked up the courage to phone her. "Hi, Barbara, what an unexpected pleasure to be speaking with you. Thelma told me you rang. I was downstairs, checking on the new production line, making sure everything was geared up to get rolling tomorrow."

"Ah, that is good news, Tim. I was calling to see how things were developing on that front. Now you've put my mind at rest that everything is still on course, I'll leave you to it. Exciting times ahead of us, Tim, don't forget that. I foresee profits going through the roof within the next few months. Stick with me, and we'll make a killing. Don't forget to get back to me about that option I shared with you about floating the company on the stock market."

"I have a lot to consider, you're going to have to bear with me on that one, Barbara."

"You've got until the end of the week. Those who hesitate and all that. We need to pounce on certain opportunities when they come our way, surely you know that by now? Maybe you don't, perhaps that's why the business has remained stagnant for the past couple of years. Well, no more, not with me at the helm."

"As a silent partner, remember?"

"Ah yes, that's a mere formality. We'll see how that pans out in the coming months. Toodle pip, for now."

He ended the call, his mind whirling up an internal cyclone. *I'm getting battered from all sides, damned if I do and damned if I bloody don't. I need to check in with Amanda and the kids.*

His wife's mobile rang and rang. All the while, the knot in his stomach grew tighter, almost cutting off his ability to breathe easily. *Where the fuck are you? Answer your goddamn phone, woman.*

"Hello, what the hell do you want? I'm busy taking care of our family. I can't be at your beck and call every time you decide to pick up the phone and ring me."

"I'm sorry, I appreciate life is hard for all of us at the moment. Is everyone okay there? Cally and Lester doing all right?"

"Yes, why? What makes today different to any other day that you felt the need to ring me and check in with us?"

"Don't be such a grouch, Amanda. I'm doing this for all of us, can't you see that?"

"You want to know what I see, husband dearest? I see our kids staring out of the window for hours on end, hoping to catch a fleeting glimpse of their father. They're on first-name terms with the postie right now, because they see more of him than they do of you, but who am I to judge? You're doing

11

all of this for us, aren't you? Well, you keep telling yourself that, and everything will be just hunky-dory in your blasted world, while ours is crumbling all around us, around me, dickhead."

Amanda hung up on him without him getting the answer he needed about Cally. He dared to ring back, but the phone rang and rang, his wife purposely ignoring it. Now he found himself in even more turmoil than before. He felt battered, being pummelled to death from all angles, in his quest to make life a better place for those around him.

Jesus, where do I go for help? What do I do to appease the person who keeps calling me, intentionally putting me on edge? What if he carries out his threat and hurts my baby? There's only one option left open to me.

CHAPTER 1

"*I* swear, if that bloody man rings me once more today, I'll snip his nuts off and hand them to Simon to grill on the barbecue at the weekend," Sally said exasperatedly, hanging up the phone.

Lorne, try as she might, couldn't hold the laughter in a moment longer. "He's a chancer. I guess he forgot about the other nine times he's called you already today."

"I know the night we showed up at his leaving do, I told him that I'd be on the end of the phone if ever he needed me, but even I have my damn limits. Jack is taking the piss. Has he contacted either you or Tony yet? You're the experts in the private investigator field, not me. Wasn't that the agreement we discussed at my house the following weekend?"

"I believe it was, and no, he hasn't rung either of us, yet. Sorry, Sal, I guess he probably feels more comfortable speaking to you than us."

"Well, he can change his ways, immediately. Otherwise, he and I are going to fall out, big time."

Lorne cringed. "Maybe give him a week or two to get into the swing of things. It's a totally different ball game, out there on your own, with no police computer database at your disposal. I found it nigh on impossible to cope with. Tony was far better at it than me, only because he was used to obtaining information covertly from unknown sources during his time working as an MI6 operative."

"We've definitely got the better deal. But Jack needs to get down and nasty and stop relying on us to do his digging for him. If the boss finds out that we're using the police system to pass details on to Jack, he won't be bloody happy."

"I agree, your ex-partner needs to learn to stand on his own two feet, it's not worth either one of us losing our careers over, but how do we tactfully tell him that?"

"That's the million-dollar question right there. Anyway, let's push that particular problem to one side for a moment and get back to the plans we were making regarding the weekend. Simon mentioned borrowing Mum and Dad's boat and going out on the river if you're up for it? We could take a couple of sleeping bags, supplies such as necessities for breakfast, and moor up outside a few pubs along the way for lunch and dinner. What do you reckon?"

Lorne shrugged. "Sounds like a great idea for all of us. I used to go on the boats with my folks when I was a youngster. Of course, it's a different kettle of fish entirely tackling the Thames, with its forty-odd locks. I think it will be far more civilised lazing the day away on the river up here, on The Broads. I bet the boys will be up for it, too, knowing how wound up the pair of them have been lately, doing their utmost to get all these properties ready to put on the market."

"That's settled then, we'll announce it to our husbands when we get home this evening."

Lorne raised a finger. "On one proviso."

"And what might that be?" Sally asked, perplexed.

"That nothing major comes our way in the meantime."

They both jumped when the phone on Sally's desk rang. They stared at each other and shook their heads.

Sally gulped and answered the phone on the third ring. "DI Sally Parker, how can I help?"

"Ah, just the person I was hoping to speak to."

Sally frowned and instinctively hit the speaker button.

The automated voice continued. "I've heard a lot about you, Inspector. How thorough you and your team are, especially where cold cases are concerned."

"That's right. We pride ourselves on having an excellent record. Who is this?"

"Come now, Inspector, you've let the side down already, asking such a dumb question only seconds into our working relationship. When it's obvious that my voice has been electronically altered for a reason. I guess I'll go elsewhere then, if you're not willing to take me seriously."

"Wait! I didn't say that. Of course I'll take you seriously. Forget I asked. Why don't you tell me why you're contacting me?"

"Now, now, Inspector, don't go thinking you're the one calling the shots around here. You're not, *I am*. Credit me with a modicum of sense, I know how these things work. You start bombarding me with inane questions while your partner, Mrs Warner there, dashes out of the room and tries to put a trace on the line. Don't bother, I've done my homework on both of you. I've also ensured this line can't get traced. It's bouncing around the world as we speak. Here we are in Hong Kong, now Italy, oops, we're off again in Australia, now back to America. Need I go on?"

"No, you've got our undivided attention. What's this call about? You can tell me that much, can't you?"

"Ah yes, indubitably. Are you ready? Pens poised over a blank sheet of paper? That is how it works, isn't it?"

"Our pens are ready for action, and you're well informed. Are you a copper? Have you been a copper in the past?"

"Goodbye, Inspector, I can see you're not willing to play this game the way it is intended. I'll find someone else to toy with, someone more compliant than you."

"No, wait. I won't say another word, not unless you prompt me, how's that?"

"Much better. I think we're going to get along well with each other."

"Good." As tempted as Sally was to ask more questions, she squeezed her lips together to suppress any words that might trip out of her mouth.

The caller remained quiet, except for taking the odd breath here and there. Sally was caught up in a torturous waiting game, the person on the other end of the line pulling her chain until finally they said, "I have news for you."

"I'm listening," Sally said tentatively.

"Go to forty-six Wellington Road in Acle. There, you will find a body, one that has been at the property for five years… maybe more, that's up to the Forensic Team to decide."

Lorne scribbled down the information in her notebook and then glanced up at Sally.

"Thank you," Sally replied. Again, dozens of questions queued up in her mind to be let loose. But she held her tongue, prepared to play the waiting game with the caller, as instructed. She needed to know who the body belonged to, and if this person knew how the body had got to be at the location. They had given her a specific time frame to work with, so the odds were that this person knew why and how the body had ended up at forty-six Wellington Road.

Suddenly the phone went dead.

"Hello? Are you still there?" Sally left the line open for a few seconds, willing the person to come back. They didn't. In the end, deflated, Sally hung up and placed her hands over her face. Dropping them after a moment or two, she shot out of her chair and said, "Come on, we need to get over there."

Lorne remained seated. A pensive expression settled on her face.

"What's wrong?"

"I wouldn't go marching into that property, not without the proper backup being actioned first."

"We can give SOCO a call en route."

Lorne raised an eyebrow. "And you think that's going to cut it? You think SOCO have nothing better to do all day than sit around and wait for us to give them a call?"

"All right, don't go there. My mind is in a vortex. I'll give Pauline a call now, see what her advice is."

"You do that. Do you want me to ask uniform to go to the location, to cordon off the property in the meantime?" Lorne asked.

"Yes, yes, you do that." Sally sank back into her chair and dialled the pathologist's number.

Lorne left the room and closed the door behind her before Sally could issue further instructions.

"Hi, Pauline, it's DI Sally Parker. Can you talk?"

"I can. It's a funny thing really, amazing that God created me with lips and a tongue to help me speak."

Sally groaned. "Responses like that aren't warranted, not at a time like this. I'm being serious. Is this a convenient moment to have a quick conversation with you or not?"

"Kind of. You've caught me between PMs. What's up? Dare I say you sound wound up about something."

"Not in the slightest... well, maybe. I've just received a call from someone with a disguised voice, that kind of put me on the back foot right away, telling me there's a dead body at a house over in Acle."

"Ah, now that is interesting. Okay, and you want me to join you at the location, is that correct?"

"Yes, if you have the time."

"Here's news for you, I'll make time. I can shove this poor lady back in the fridge and deal with her later. Now, I need you to understand something, I wouldn't do this for just anyone."

"I'm extremely and eternally grateful to you for altering things to suit me."

"I wouldn't go as far as to say that to *suit me* would be the correct term, after all, I'm eager to find out what's going on myself. The automated voice is an intriguing element to this case, wouldn't you say?"

"I agree. Which is why I'm keen to get over there ASAP."

"You'd better supply the address then."

Sally gave her the details.

"Ah, okay, well, we should get there around the same time. I'll inform SOCO, see if they have any spare bodies they can send, as well."

"That's great, thanks, Pauline."

"See you there shortly."

Pauline hung up, putting an end to the conversation.

Sally pushed back her chair and went in search of her partner. Lorne was at her desk, staring at her computer screen.

"Everything all right, Lorne?"

"Christ, you scared the crap… sneaking up on me like that."

"I didn't. What are you up to?"

"I rang the desk sergeant. He's sent a car out to the location to secure the scene. Rather than wait around, doing bugger all, I thought I'd do a search on who owns the property. According to the electoral register, the property owner died two years ago, and the house has remained empty ever since."

"Great, I wonder what state it's going to be in."

"I suppose we're going to find out soon enough. Want me to trawl back, see who the previous owners have been over the years?"

"No, pass it over to Joanna. We need to get on the road. Pauline and her team are on the way over to the house now."

"You were lucky to get hold of them and for her to be so accommodating." Lorne stood and walked the length of the room to give Joanna the information she had to hand, so far.

"I caught her between PMs. She's as keen to find out what's going on as we are. Glad to see her finally coming around to our way of thinking."

Lorne smiled. "It's taken her long enough."

"We'll hopefully be back soon, folks. Crack on with the other tasks we've got on the go until we return. Let's ensure the decks are clear in case there's something to this call. Of course, it could turn out to be some perverted hoax."

"We'll know soon enough," Lorne replied.

She pushed through the swing doors, and Sally caught up with her on the stairs.

"Indeed. This is all your fault, you realise that, don't you?" Sally said.

Lorne paused mid-step and looked at her. "Huh? How do you work that one out?"

"Weren't we discussing plans for the weekend when that blasted call came in?"

They laughed and continued on their journey.

"Always the same. Tempting fate has a habit of biting us in the arse."

PAULINE and the SOCO team beat them to the address. As requested, the area had been cordoned off by crime scene tape, and a SOCO tech had gained access to the house via the lounge window that had been left unlocked.

"Sloppy, leaving the window unsecured," Sally said. She slipped into her paper suit and glanced back at the house. "I bet it's a tip inside, judging by the flaking paint on the outside and the state of the garden, if you can call it that."

"Yeah, not sure I would go that far, a jungle more like," Lorne replied. She jumped up and down on the spot, pulling the suit up to her crotch. "Damn things. You have to be fit to even consider getting into one."

"I agree. They don't make it easy. Right, let's see what kind of mood Pauline is in. She seemed to be all right when I last spoke to her, but, as we both know, her moods can change in an instant."

"PMA."

They joined Pauline at the back of her van.

She was collecting a few necessities before she entered the house. "Hi, we haven't been inside yet, so I haven't got a clue what to expect once we're in there."

"Not long to wait now."

The three of them entered the small garden. The path had large crater-like cracks that forced them to pick their way carefully to the front door without going over on their ankles. Sally had already shown her ID to the officer standing guard at the front door before she'd tackled getting into her suit. He opened the door to allow them access to the house.

The musty smell hit them.

"Jesus, we're going to need to wear a mask, aren't we?" Sally said.

Pauline didn't hang around. She jumped over a few of the cracks in the path and returned to her van where she collected three gas masks.

"Damn, that's a bit over the top, isn't it? I hate wearing one of those," Lorne complained.

"I'm with you on that," Sally said, "but what's the alternative? It bloody reeks in there."

Lorne shrugged and slipped on her mask when Pauline rejoined them.

"Here you go, ladies. I took a punt that you wouldn't have any of these in the car."

"You're right, they're not standard issue. Thanks, we owe you, Pauline."

"You do. Enough of this messing about, let's get inside."

They covered their shoes, then Sally and Lorne followed the pathologist into the gloomy hallway. The weather being just as dreary as the interior didn't help much either. Sally flicked the switch at the bottom of the stairs, chancing her luck. Nothing.

"Wishful thinking on your part," Lorne said.

"Worth a try. Where shall we start?" Sally asked.

Pauline gestured towards the rear of the house, to the kitchen area. "Out here seems as good a place as any." On the way through the hallway, she pointed out a couple of doors to her right. "Under-the-stairs storage perhaps, and this one could be a cellar, with endless possibilities."

Sally shuddered. "Don't, I can't stand cellars. Lorne, didn't you have a case back in London where you found several bodies buried in a cellar?"

"You've got a good memory. Yep, not a very pleasant discovery. As I recall, we arrested a vile couple who killed several tradesmen who had worked on their house."

"Definitely some warped, sick individuals around," Sally muttered.

The kitchen dated back to the sixties. Large, patterned tiles stood out between the turquoise-blue cupboards at the bottom and the white wall cupboards.

"I dread to think how people would react if this style ever came back into fashion," Lorne said.

"Yeah, definitely not my cup of tea. Can't see anything being in here, can you?" Sally asked.

Lorne opened a few of the lower cupboards to check. "That's a negative. Don't think I'll bother with the top ones; they'd soon fall off the wall if a dead body was stuffed inside."

Pauline led the way out of the room and paused by the back door. Through the glass pane, she pointed to a shed at the bottom of the garden. "Might be worth a look later, if nothing shows up in the house."

Along the hallway was the dining room, which consisted of a table and four fabric-covered chairs also dating back to the sixties, possibly the seventies. Scattered around the room were several filled boxes.

"Someone packing up ready to leave, perhaps?" Sally suggested.

"Maybe," Lorne agreed. "If it wasn't used daily, then it seems logical to put the excess boxes in here, out of the way."

They went back into the hallway and entered the lounge. Minimal furniture on view in there. Two armchairs and a leather Chesterfield completed the suite that appeared to be in good condition, despite its age. Again, there were a few boxes tucked into the corner, along with a bureau-cum-drinks cabinet along the far wall. A portable TV on a pine table stood off to the left of the gas fire standing in front of the chimney breast.

"Again, nothing out of the ordinary in here," Sally said. "That only leaves upstairs and the cellar to check."

"I bet it's in the latter," Lorne grumbled.

"We'll see." Pauline led the way up the creaking staircase. "Mind your step. Try and keep to the side instead of using the middle, ladies," she called over her shoulder.

The creaking lessened once they changed their route. The first room they came across was small and filled with boxes from floor to ceiling.

"Nothing to see in there, not unless the contents of the boxes need to be examined," Pauline said.

Sally noticed the glint in the pathologist's eye and tutted. "Don't even go there. A house full of body parts; you're giving me the willies."

The next room consisted of a single bed with a nylon bedspread, again popular in the sixties and seventies.

"I'm getting the impression the occupant probably lived here their whole life and wasn't keen on updating either their furniture or their surroundings, judging by the flock wallpaper we've come across in every room," Pauline noted.

"I agree. Our team is checking out the facts about the owner as we speak. That leaves the main bedroom to tackle," Sally said.

Pauline swept into the room first after giving the bathroom next door a cursory glance. "Ah okay, well, this is a likely place to find something, especially as we've written off every other room in the house for various reasons." She removed her mask and inhaled a large breath. Then replaced her mask again, much to Sally's amazement.

"Are you mad? What the fuck are you doing?" Sally asked.

"It's obvious, isn't it? I'm seeing if the smell has intensified coming upstairs. It's not surprising if the owner was bedbound. I'm not saying the stench is to do with rotting flesh, especially after five years, but..." Pauline replied.

"And has it? Not that I have any intention of finding out for myself."

Lorne shocked Sally by copying Pauline and also removing her mask, which she swiftly replaced. The viewing panel quickly steamed up as her breathing notched up a little.

"Maybe Lorne can answer that." Pauline smirked.

Lorne gagged then said, "I'd say that is an affirmative."

"You two are gluttons for punishment." Sally scanned the room, searching for possible hiding places, and her gaze

23

stopped on the most obvious, the wardrobe. She pointed at the bank of mahogany-coloured louver doors along the back wall.

Lorne took the hint and opened the closest door to her. "Nothing in here."

Sally checked the cupboard at the other end. "Nothing here either."

They met in the middle after examining the other wardrobes, and both shook their heads.

"Nothing untoward in any of them, not unless the body has been cut up," Lorne said.

"It's something that we need to consider, unless…" Pauline started to say.

"Unless?" Sally prompted. She eyed Pauline curiously as the pathologist's gaze ran the length and breadth of the room.

"In the walls," Pauline said matter-of-factly.

"What?" Sally and Lorne said in unison.

"Obviously we're going to need to search the room thoroughly before we get down and dirty and start removing the walls, that's always a last resort."

Lorne looked up. "Hang on, what about above us? In the loft?"

Pauline nodded. "Again, that's a possibility we should consider. Hang on." She went to the door and called down the stairs to a member of her team. "Dan, can you hear me? The smell is more intense up here. It's either coming from the main bedroom or there could be something lingering in the attic. Have you got a ladder to hand?"

"I'll get one from the van, be right back."

Pauline returned to the room. "Good call, Lorne. We should know either way soon enough."

Sally glanced down at the ancient carpet. "What about under the floorboards?"

"Unlikely, given the gap between floors," Lorne replied.

"I agree, although we should never rule anything out," Pauline said.

The clatter of a ladder caught their attention, and Dan appeared in the doorway, his face free from any accessories.

"Jesus, guess I'd better fetch a mask. I thought I'd get away with it, but the stench up here is unbelievable. I'll be right back."

Pauline tutted as the tech disappeared and the creaking of the stairs filled the room. "Idiot," she muttered.

Sally suppressed a chuckle. "You crack me up."

Dan reappeared. The three ladies moved towards the doorway and watched Dan set up the ladder below the loft hatch. He opened it and entered the attic. They heard him scrambling over things in the cavity above and then cry out.

"Shit, I wasn't expecting that."

"What was it?" Pauline bellowed.

"A bloody rake up here. I stood on the head, and the handle sprang up and smacked me in the face."

Pauline shook her head and repeated the same word under her breath, "Idiot," then shouted, "Anything else up there?"

"Lots of boxes and general tat that you usually find in an attic, like suitcases."

"Can you open them? Or are they locked?"

"Let me have a look," Dan hollered back.

Sally suspected his exertions could be heard two streets away.

"Nope, nothing in the two I can open. There's a third one, but it's quite small in comparison, so I wouldn't hold out much hope with that one either."

"Okay, is there anything else of interest?" Pauline shouted. "Dare you take your mask off, see if the smell is worse up there?"

"No, it's hard to say. In parts it's worse and in other areas it's less, so I'd say about the same."

Pauline hit the doorframe of the bedroom and rolled her eyes at Sally. "I'm working with bloody... nope, I refuse to say it a third time, you get my drift."

"We do," Sally confirmed. "So that leaves the walls then, doesn't it?"

Pauline nodded. "Seems logical. I'll get the team started on them ASAP. Do you want to hang around?"

Sally glanced at Lorne and shrugged. "It's not like we have anything else to do, do we?"

Her partner smiled. "Fine by me. At least we'll find out first-hand if we stick around."

"Exactly. Do you need us to stick around?" Sally asked.

"No, let's leave it to the experts. It won't be a smash-and-grab thing, the walls will have to be taken apart bit by bit and catalogued. It's usually a slow process."

"On second thoughts, maybe it won't be a wise move hanging around here," Sally said.

"What about if we have a chat with the neighbours?" Lorne proposed.

"Good idea. We'll call back after we've spoken to the neighbours on both sides," Sally told Pauline.

"No rush, we'll be at it for a while."

Sally and Lorne left the house and stripped off their suits which they placed into the black sack outside the front door. They put the masks in the back of Pauline's van for later.

"Want to stick together or split up?" Lorne asked.

"We might as well do it together. It's not like we're in a race against time, for a change."

They decided to knock on the door to the right of forty-six first. There was an elderly woman staring out of the front window. Sally waved and pointed at the door. The woman smiled, not an ounce of embarrassment seeping into her features. The door opened within seconds.

"Hello, dears. How can I be of assistance to you today?"

Sally and Lorne flashed their IDs.

"DI Sally Parker, and this is my partner, DS Lorne Warner. Would it be okay if we came in and spoke with you, Mrs...?"

"It's Joyce Greenall. Yes, of course. Oh my, I don't recall ever having the police in my house before. Come in, dears. Would you like a cuppa? I don't mind, I've always got the kettle on."

"A coffee would be lovely, thank you." Sally stepped into the hallway.

Lorne closed the door behind her.

"You go into the lounge. I won't be a tick. Sugar and milk?"

"Milk and one sugar in each of them, thanks," Sally replied.

She and Lorne entered the lounge which was more up to date than the one in the house next door. True to her word, Joyce joined them a few minutes later with a plate full of rich tea biscuits and two cups and saucers which she handed to Sally and Lorne after they'd taken a seat on the Dralon-covered sofa.

"Have you lived here long, Joyce?" Sally asked.

"About ten years. I've made a few changes in that time, unlike my neighbour, but you'll have noticed that already, I should imagine."

"You could say that." Sally smiled. "What can you tell us about the owners next door?"

"It belonged to Nancy Hart. Can I ask why you've shown up out of the blue like this?"

"We're checking the house as something major has come to our attention. I'm sorry, I can't go into detail about that for now, not until something has been confirmed by the tech team searching the property at the moment."

"Sounds intriguing. I wonder what that can be after all these years."

Sally inclined her head. "Perhaps you can tell us what happened to Nancy?"

"It was terrible. She had dementia and was left to die all alone in that house a couple of years ago. I did my bit to help out when I could, but it wasn't my responsibility to care for the old woman. I feel bad saying that but at the time I wasn't very well myself, my own health was deteriorating through a heart problem. Later that year, I had to have open-heart surgery."

"I'm sorry to hear that. I'm glad you helped out Nancy when you could."

"Oh, I did. I couldn't sit in here and think about her suffering the way she was. Her family couldn't have cared less. She had carers coming in four times a day and spent the rest of her time in bed. No bugger deserves to be treated like that." Tears welled up, and Joyce plucked a tissue from a nearby box and dabbed at her eyes.

"Did her family live far away? Or did they live locally and just not care?"

"Down south somewhere. Not sure if she left a will or not. If she did, and they were mentioned in it, I've not seen hide nor hair of them in the time since she passed. She was such a dear, sweet old lady."

"I have to ask why she wasn't put in a home."

"I asked the same thing, every time I spoke to the carers, and they couldn't tell me. Heartbreaking, it was. She couldn't remember a soul, often cried out during the night. I would go tearing around there and check the house over for her, but there was never anyone there, not from what I could tell. I had a chat with a doctor once, collared him outside when he was visiting, and he told me she was prone to halluci-nating and put it down to the dementia. Again, it broke my heart in two to consider her all alone twenty-four hours a day, but I suppose it's a sign of the times. We've become a selfish society. Most people don't care for anyone else other than themselves."

"I would hope that statement isn't true for most of us, maybe a select few, but I wouldn't say it was widespread."

Joyce stared at her, her eyes narrowed. "You believe what you want to believe, and I'll continue to live in the real world. Listen to all the horror stories of nurses killing babies et cetera. It's a truly wicked world we live in, and I don't see it changing anytime soon."

Sally and Lorne looked at each other.

Sally cleared the lump in her throat and said, "It's a tough call. I agree, she should have been treated better. Maybe the system failed her. None of us really know the answer to that, do we?"

"I do. Yes, you're right, the system did fail her. People need to be held to account for letting that poor woman down. She had no one to fight her battles. I did what I could, within reason. I have to live with the guilt of knowing that I could have done more to have helped her."

Sally held a hand up to stop Joyce from saying more. "No, I'm sorry, but I can't sit here and listen to you feeling guilty for something that was totally out of your hands. You've said yourself that you were drastically ill at the time. It wasn't your responsibility to look after your neighbour."

"I've heard every side of the argument over the years, but nothing anyone can say will alter my opinion. According to the carers who came every day to see her, there are thou-sands of people living like this, day in, day out. It has to stop. What is that saying about our society? I apologise, I don't mean to take this out on you, but something needs to change.

29

This country can't keep allowing people, *outsiders* from other countries to come here, expecting state handouts when the UK neglect their own elderly people, born and raised here, who have paid their whole working lives into a system that is going to eventually fail them when they become old and infirm."

Sally shrugged. "You're right. I don't know what else I can say or do to change the situation."

"I know that. Again, I'm sorry, but I needed to vent, and you've taken the brunt of my frustration. Deep down it's my guilt surfacing for letting poor Nancy down."

There was nothing else Sally could say to appease the woman. She found herself lost for words.

"Joyce, perhaps you can tell us why there are boxes all over the house?" Lorne jumped in to help Sally out.

Sally released a relieved sigh and sipped at her coffee to try to regain her composure.

"Ah yes, I was guilty of packing her things up, after her death. I thought it might help the family out when they finally came to reclaim the house, but no one ever showed up. Which has left me scratching my head on more than one occasion."

"That explains at least one puzzle in the house," Sally replied.

"I still don't understand why you're here. Why now? Two years that poor lady has been gone."

Sally shook her head. "I'm sorry, we can't tell you that, not at the moment."

Joyce sat back and crossed her arms. "Two can play at that game."

And there it was, this old lady holding them to ransom.

"You're not being fair, Joyce. I'm afraid I can't reveal any further information."

"Then it's time for you to drink up and get out of my

house. It's not good to have too much stress in my life, not at my age."

Sally replaced her half-drunk coffee on the tray and stood. "Sorry you feel that way. We'll have a chat with some of your neighbours, see if they're willing to help us with our enquiries."

"Oh, sit down, you silly woman. I was only joshing with you. Why is it that people take everything so seriously these days?"

Sally laughed. "Consider me told. It's not that I don't want to tell you, it's that there is nothing really to tell, not yet."

"Well, then that's different. It doesn't make sense, but at least you've told me the truth. Is there anything else you need to know?"

Sally grinned. "Plenty, if you have the time and are willing and able to cast your mind back a few years."

"There's nothing wrong with my mind. I told my daughter that if ever dementia came knocking on my door, she needs to do away with me. Put a bottle of pills in my hand and be done with it. I could never go through what poor Nancy had to put up with. I truly wouldn't wish that on my worst enemy. It's a degrading and an undignified way to die that has no place in this world. If scientists can come up with a vaccine for Covid within a month or whatever it was, then why, oh why, can't they come up with an answer for Alzheimer's and cancer? That's blooming beyond me and puzzles me every time I see anything about dementia on the TV. Wicked, wicked disease. Sorry, I shouldn't have spouted such twaddle, you're not here to listen to me raving about the wrongs in this world. Oh, and don't get me started on climate change, that's another subject that gets me riled up."

"I read somewhere that scientists had been working on a vaccine against coronaviruses for years, so the knowledge gained helped speed up the development. However, you have a right to feel aggrieved if what you saw unsettled you, and yes, I totally agree with you about climate change and the lack of interest in the subject from certain world leaders. That aside, going back to Nancy's relatives, I don't suppose you have any contact details for them, do you? A phone number or an address, perhaps? Even if it's an old one."

Joyce wriggled in her chair to the edge of her seat and eventually got to her feet. She crossed the room to a wooden cabinet in the corner and opened the top drawer. After searching through the contents, she removed a small address book and rifled through it a few times. "I know what you're thinking, why isn't it an A-Z one? That's because my husband bought this on a whim because he liked the pretty picture on the front, and I began filling it up, without much thought at the time. It's only in later life that it's turned out to be a huge source of frustration for me."

"We're in no rush," Sally insisted.

"Ah, here it is. Ronald Edgar, twenty-two Frobisher Avenue, Shiphay in Torquay, in Devon."

Lorne jotted down the details. "Any idea how long ago that would have been?"

Joyce brought the book back to her seat and sat. She placed a hand to her cheek and mulled the question over for a few moments. "I wouldn't like to say, maybe just after I moved in here, so possibly about ten years ago. I don't think you'd be far wrong with that assumption."

"Would you happen to have his phone number as well?" Sally asked.

"No, I checked that, there's nothing written down."

"Not to worry. I think you've given us more than enough to be going on with. Was Ronald her son?"

"Oh no, he was her nephew. I've only ever seen him the once. He came up for a fleeting visit on his way up to Scotland, made a detour to see her from what I can recall."

32

"We'll see if we can track him down. No other relatives that you know about?"

"I don't think so, no. Hang on a moment, I think I have the name of Nancy's solicitor in my book somewhere, if you'll give me a few seconds to find it."

"Of course. It would be really useful if you had that."

They waited patiently, and again Joyce came up with the goods.

"Here we are, Charter and Sons, they're in Acle itself. Not too far from here. It might be worth you calling in to see what they have to say about the will and its contents."

"We'll definitely drop by and see them. See, you've been extremely helpful, despite your doubts."

"I'm glad you think so. Is there something in the house? Is that why you're raiding the place? Drugs or something along those lines?"

"Again, I can't say, not yet. I'm sorry, I'm not intentionally keeping you in the dark, I promise. Right, we're going to get out of your hair now. I want to thank you once again for all the information you've given us."

"It's the least I could do. I hope it helps you find her nephew, I really do. He should be made to sit down in a police station and told about her death in all its gory details. Bloody deserting her like that. Shame on him."

Rather than keep going over old ground with the elderly woman, Sally stood, and Lorne followed her to the door.

"Stay where you are, we can let ourselves out."

"As you wish."

"The neighbour on the other side, have they lived there long?"

"No, they're relatively new. They arrived after Nancy passed away. Let me think now… no, actually, those who knew her well have all either departed this world or are now residing in a care home. Not sure any of them will be of much use to you, as such."

"That's fine. Again, thanks for your assistance, Joyce. Enjoy the rest of your day. Hopefully the tech team won't disturb you too much next door."

"You mean they're likely to?"

"Possibly. Leave it with me. It was lovely meeting you. Take care of yourself."

"You, too. I feel I should say good luck, even if you have left me in the dark a little."

Sally smiled and exited the room. In the hallway, as Lorne closed the lounge door, Sally whispered, "Me and my big mouth, I swear it'll be the death of me one of these days."

"You're being too hard on yourself. Where are we off to now? The solicitors?"

"By the sounds of it, I think it'll be a waste of time hanging around here, knocking on doors, if those who knew her best have all moved on."

"Agreed."

CHAPTER 2

 *ack in 2018*

EVERYTHING WAS GOING full steam ahead with the new production line. Barbara had made an appearance herself, once the line was up and running and, to Tim, she seemed just as enthusiastic about it as he was, which had surprised him. Matthew had kept his distance until the day he left and needed to be prised from his office when anything new happened on the factory floor, and then it had to be something of magnitude that caught his interest.

"Keep up the good work. The girls seem to have developed a good rhythm already, Tim, so if they're happy with the way things are progressing so far then we should be, too," Barbara said.

"I'm delighted. As you say, if they're happy then there's no reason why we shouldn't be." *Maybe it might be worth upping production even more, if they're too comfortable with their workload.*

The office staff each took it in turns to visit the production line at Tim's request. He was keen for everyone to see history in the making. This line was going to be producing goods likely to save the factory and keep everyone in a job. Pride swelled along with adrenaline through his veins. Eva, one of the secretaries, brought him a mug of coffee while he stood in the doorway, watching the filled boxes come off the production line.

"Thanks, Eva. This is probably one of the greatest days of my life."

"I can imagine. I'm proud watching it and I had nothing to do with getting the factory to this point, unlike you. What about your wife? Shouldn't she be down here to witness this epic day?"

"Sadly, she doesn't rate the factory as highly as I do. This type of thing wouldn't get her excited, not as much as it does me, but that's fine. She's busy dealing with the kids and seeing to their daily needs."

"That's a shame. I bet that sucks now and again, her lack of interest, I mean?"

He shrugged. He couldn't deny it, Eva had hit the nail on the head with her observation. "I'm used to flying the flag alone around here. Most of the time, Matthew couldn't have given a toss either."

"The new boss, Barbara, seems like she's going to give you all the support you need from now on, Tim. You must be pleased about that?"

He peered over his shoulder, leaned in and whispered, "Between you and me, I hope she lives up to her position and remains a silent partner. Don't get me wrong, I'm grateful she showed up here today, even if it was only for a fleeting visit, but I have to say I was relieved when she left half an hour later."

"I can understand what you're saying. You're used to

everything running smoothly, with you at the helm, so it's unnerving when someone comes along and begins looking over your shoulder."

Tim winked and tapped the side of his nose with his index finger. "You've got that right. Anyway, you should be getting back to work, and I need to venture outside, make sure the packing department is running as smoothly as the production line. If it isn't, things will soon grind to a halt in here, and we can't have that, can we?"

"I'll leave it in your capable hands. Congratulations once again, Tim. You deserve all the success and more that is coming your way."

"Thanks, Eva. That's very kind of you to say so." With that, he pushed through the clear plastic doors to the packaging area. "How are you doing out here, Sid?" he asked the man who had been with him virtually from day one.

"Couldn't be better, sir. I told you that you should have done this years ago, didn't I? But would you listen to me?"

Tim smiled and raised his hands in the air. "Hey, you're not going to get any arguments from me, not after witnessing the success of the line for the last few hours. How long before the first truck is ready to hit the road? I'm desperate for the buyers to get their hands on the new range and get it out there on the shelves. The sooner the public have access to the bars the better. It'll only mean one thing…"

"More orders. I've tasted it, you know I'm not that bothered about chocolate usually, but I have to say, sir, this has winner written all over it, and rightly so."

"You're very kind, Sid. Let's hope you're right. We could do with some good luck after the tumultuous past few years we've been through."

"Yes, there was talk about you jumping ship as well as Matthew, closing this place down. I told people they were talking out of their ars... umm backsides. It wouldn't have come to that, would it?"

Tim heaved out a sigh as the past couple of excruciating years flashed before his eyes. "It may well have, if this line hadn't popped into my head, Sid. We'll see how it goes. Maybe if this product is a success, then I'll consider putting in the extra work and coming up with more to add to the range."

Sid wagged a finger. "Don't go getting ahead of yourself, sir, one step at a time. You barely see your family as it is, without heaping yet more stress on your shoulders. Do you ever get to see anything of the outside world nowadays?"

Tim chewed his lip and sighed. "Perhaps you're right, maybe I should quash my enthusiasm for a while, see how the line is received by the general public for at least a month or two."

"You'd do right to do that, sir. All this has been a huge weight on your shoulders. I don't have to be no Einstein to see what effect this has all had on your health over the last few months. None of it will be worth it if you put yourself in an early grave."

"Christ, don't write me off just yet, man."

"Ah, sorry, I didn't mean to. I was adding a word of caution, that's all."

"Noted, and I've taken all of your advice on board. You're a good man, Sid. And I meant what I said last week, if we can get all the wagons loaded and out on the road in a timely manner today, there's a large bonus coming your way."

"Thanks, but I really don't need it. You pay me to do a job which I intend to carry out efficiently and to the best of my ability. You deserve all the success that is on the cards for you this week, you've worked your bollocks off over the years. Sorry, excuse my language, but you have. I've always admired your work ethic, often putting this place before your family life. That couldn't have been easy for you."

"It wasn't. Hopefully, if this range takes off, I'll be able to employ more competent staff, some more of your standing in the future, with the intention of taking a step back."

Sid's eyebrows rose and fell. "Hmm... well, we'll have to see if that comes to fruition, eh?"

They both laughed. Tim slapped the older man on the shoulder and entered the factory again. He stood beside the production line, this being the proudest day of his forty years of walking this earth, his heart swelling to a new level until his mobile vibrated in his jacket pocket.

He pulled himself away from the captivating sight and, once he was in the hallway where it was much quieter, he answered the phone. "Hello, Timothy Farrant, how can I help?" He noticed it was from a withheld number.

"Ah, Timothy, lad. How's it going today?"

Tim squeezed his eyes shut, recognising the voice. He gulped down the saliva filling his mouth and said, "It's going well, all things considered. What do you want?"

"You went back on our deal. I warned you what would happen if production increased today, didn't I?"

"Umm... it was a case of needs must. I had to up the output, get the new line out there today or the factory would have folded, it's as simple as that."

"Simple as that, eh? Say hello to some guests I have with me."

"Tim... what's going on? Who are these people, and why are they holding me and the children?"

At the sound of his wife's terrified voice, Tim slammed against the wall behind him, his legs wobbling, almost giving way beneath him. "Amanda, has he hurt you?"

"No. Lester tried to put up a fight, to protect me and Cally, but one of the men jabbed him in the stomach. He doubled over. I hated seeing my baby hurt like that. What do they want, Tim? Does this have something to do with the factory?"

He ran a hand around his face, unsure what to say or do next in case it upset the kidnappers and they vented their frustrations on his family. "I'm sorry, Amanda, I don't know what they want."

"Don't listen to him, Amanda, it's all lies. He was under strict instructions not to let the production of the new range go ahead, and yet here we are, on launch day, the bars swiftly being processed by all accounts."

"I had to do this, to save the company, we were going under," Tim explained, his words tumbling out of his mouth before he had a chance to realise the jeopardy he was putting his family in.

"That was the whole point, we wanted your company to fold. Now... well, now, you've only got yourself to blame for putting your family's lives at risk."

Amanda screamed in the distance, and then his two kids yelled out for their mother.

"What the...? No, please, you can't hurt them, they're all I've got."

"Apart from that damn factory of yours, you mean, don't you?"

"No, the factory no longer matters, not now you've got my family. Tell me what you need from me. I'll ensure I put this right. Please, I want to make amends, you have to allow me to do that. Let them go. Take me in exchange for them."

"Stop telling me what to do. You had your chance to prevent this from happening and you sat back in that executive chair of yours and did fuck all. Well, now you're going to suffer the consequences... or they are, your wife and children. Sweet Cally, such an adorable little girl..."

"No, don't you lay a hand on her... on any of them. Tell me what you want, and I'll comply with your wishes."

"Talk is cheap. You had your chance and you screwed it up. The perils that lie ahead of your family are going to be that much greater now because of your lacklustre ability to do what was asked of you... to stop the production line."

"I'll do it now, it's not too late. No chocolate bars have hit the road yet."

"Nope, it's far too late. Let things go, for now. I'll get back to you with further instructions when the time is right."

"No, you can't do this. You can't kidnap my family and then leave me high and dry, you just can't."

"And who is going to stop me?" The man laughed. "Not you. You're so wrapped up in your own little world that nothing else matters, does it? If it did, we wouldn't be in this situation today, would we? Yes, you're to blame for everything."

"I want to put things right. Let me stop the production. My new partner will be livid, but I'm willing to work around that if it means I get my family back alive."

"There are no guarantees in this life, as you know. The trouble is, I haven't decided what I'm going to do with your family yet, but you carry on with the way things are running there, that's obviously at the top of your agenda right now."

"It's not. I'm going to halt things."

"Do what you want. I'll get back to you soon with further instructions."

The kidnapper ended the call, leaving Tim staring at his phone. A member of the packing team entered the hallway and saw him standing there, teetering on an abyss.

"Tim, is everything okay?"

"Yes, yes, everything is fine. Get back to work," he snapped, instantly regretting his harsh words.

He needed to get out of there. He patted his jacket pocket,

searching for his keys. Although he'd spoken to Amanda, he still needed to check his family had gone. He drove the five miles to his house at breakneck speed, his fingers metaphorically crossed all the way that a police car didn't spot him and pull him over.

Barging through the front door of their smart mansion, the one he had commissioned to be custom-built for them a few years earlier, when things were going well before the recent decline in production, he was confronted by dozens of clown balloons popping up here and there in every room he entered. Some of them had pictures of his family's faces on, with a speech bubble that cried out for help. His heart shattered into tiny pieces at the thought of this person, more than one if what Amanda had said during their conversation was true, having his family at their mercy. He tried to block out the vile images of his wife and children being hurt by the kidnappers.

Withdrawing his phone, he thought about calling the number back, forgetting that it had been withheld. *What the fuck does that mean? How am I supposed to get in touch with them?* He scanned the room, popped some of the more offensive balloons and lashed out at the others as he blazed a trail through the house, tears cascading down his cheeks. It was only just hitting him now, the danger his family were in, after coming here and seeing what these people were capable of. Invading his home. Swooping in and kidnapping his wife and children without them realising the kind of danger they were in. What the fuck did he do about the situation? Go to the police? How many times had he read over the years what that amounted to? Getting the police involved would surely sign Amanda's and the kids' death certificates, wouldn't it?

How do I get us out of this mess? First, they tell me to stop the production of the new range, then they tell me not to bother. What's that all about?

He ran upstairs and entered the master bedroom. There, lying on the bed was a dummy, tied to the headboard, a picture of his wife's face attached to the head. The image was too much for him to take. He collapsed to his knees and rocked back and forth, his hands covering his face, mopping up his genuine tears of grief. "What have I done?"

CHAPTER 3

Sally and Lorne entered the solicitor's office. Mr Yates was expecting them after Lorne had rung ahead to make sure he would be available to speak with them.

The young blonde receptionist invited them to take a seat while she checked if Yates was ready to receive them. "That's fine, he's asked me to take you through. If you'd like to come this way."

They followed her up a narrow, grey-carpeted corridor to the office at the rear. A man in his fifties stood to greet them as they entered. He shook their hands and invited them to take a seat.

"Would you like a drink?"

"We're fine, thanks all the same," Sally said.

He nodded and dismissed the receptionist. Once they were alone, he interlocked his fingers and placed his hands on the desk in front of him. "How can I help you? You mentioned something about Nancy Hart's house?"

"Yes, we'd like to know more about her family, if you can help us out?"

"Her family? Right, let me pull up the file on my computer. It should be in the tab here. I got it ready for you when you rang earlier, just to save us some time. May I ask what your interest is in the family?"

Sally scratched her head, unsure what to tell Yates when there was very little she knew as yet. "I received a call earlier today, telling me that something could be found at the address," Sally said, being as loose as possible with the facts.

Yates frowned. "Come now, Inspector, you're going to have to be more forthcoming than that."

"Sorry, I can't give you any further information than that at present. SOCO are currently going through the house as we speak. Until they find some concrete evidence, then I'm not willing to commit further."

"Sounds ominous. Are we talking about a body?"

Sally was taken aback that he would come to that conclusion as swiftly as he had. "What makes you say that, sir?"

"Ha, credit me with some sense. Why else would SOCO be involved?"

Sally shrugged and inhaled a breath. "Okay, you've got me there. Can we disregard that at the moment? What can you tell me about the family, if anything?"

"If you insist. Let me think about this." He fell silent and reread the file on his screen. "Ah yes, one relative, I believe, a Ronald Edgar who I contacted at the time of her death."

"And what happened about the house?"

"I don't know. As far as I'm concerned it was transferred into his name and then... just a moment, let me recheck the file... yes, here it is. Unfortunately, Ronald died a year after his aunt."

"Bugger, I mean, oh no, that's a shame. So, what happens to the house now?"

"Out of my hands now that it has nothing to do with my

client. You're going to need to do some digging into Mr Edgar's estate, see if it went to probate or not."

Sally groaned. "That could take us a while to sort out."

"It might, yes."

"You don't happen to know if Edgar had any other living relatives, do you?"

He shook his head and tutted. "Nothing on file. I'm not sure what else I can tell you."

"You've given us more than we thought we would obtain, thank you, Mr Yates. Sorry to interrupt your day."

"Glad to be of service. Sorry the news wasn't better."

Sally shook his hand, and she and Lorne left his office.

"Great, what do we do now?" Lorne mumbled on their way back to the reception area.

"We chase up the information in the hope that another family member comes to the surface."

"And if they don't?"

"We need to think positively, Lorne. If we don't, we'll fall at the first hurdle. Let's head back to the house, see if they've uncovered anything there, yet."

TEN MINUTES LATER, with a fresh set of protectives on, Sally and Lorne entered the house once more to find the main bedroom filled with plaster dust and a gaping hole in one of the walls.

"We're back, none the wiser. Actually, that's not quite true. The house was left to a Ronald Edgar, a nephew of the deceased. He died a year later, so we need to do some digging to establish who owns the property now."

"Could it still be going through probate?" Pauline asked. "These things have a tendency to linger on for months, if not years."

"Something we need to look into. How's it going here?"

"We're making lots of mess and getting nowhere fast, but what's new with cases such as this? I'm sure it's only a matter of time before we find something."

Sally scanned the room. "Wouldn't it be better to start in different areas? Why limit yourself to just that one wall which has proved to be pointless so far?"

Pauline and her team of techs all stared at Sally. She wished the ground would swallow her up where she stood.

"You might want to rephrase that, DI Parker," Pauline suggested.

"I... er... didn't mean anything derogatory by it. Bugger. I'll keep my mouth shut in future. As you were."

Lorne sniggered behind her. Sally spun around and looked daggers at her. Lorne pulled the hood of her suit down, covering the window in her gas mask.

Sally turned back and cleared her throat. "Umm... let's get past this awkward moment. Is there anything we can do while we're here?"

"You can stop asking insulting questions, that would be a bonus. Apart from that, nothing. A scene such as this can't be rushed, I told you that earlier. It's no good you marching in here demanding to know what's happening every five minutes of the day, it's only going to hinder our progress."

"Okay," Sally replied sheepishly and retreated to the hallway.

Lorne joined her. "Don't take it to heart, she's right, even though she could have said it more diplomatically."

Sally gazed out of the spare bedroom window at the house next door. "I know, she's only doing her job. What would you do in my shoes?" she asked, suddenly doubting herself. She'd apparently been doing that a lot since Jack had left and Lorne had filled his shoes. *I know I'm being ridiculous but...*

"You don't need me to tell you what to do next, Sal. Don't let Pauline knock your confidence, you're better than that."

"Am I? I'm not so sure."

Lorne grabbed her upper arms and shook her. "You are. There's nothing more we can do around here. Why don't we go somewhere, have a coffee and a chat?"

"Because we're snowed under, or we should be. There's something here, we can all sense it, but that's all the information we have to hand at present. We should have more."

"Why should we? This case dropped into our laps barely a couple of hours ago. You're not being fair on yourself, but more than that, you're questioning the team's abilities as well. Sorry, I won't allow you to do that."

Sally stared out of the window, her mind whirling but her mouth as dry as a bone. In the end, she shouted, "See you later, Pauline. Ring me if you find anything, and I'll come back."

"You do that. I hope you return in a better mood than you're leaving in."

Lorne gave Sally a nudge when she stopped dead in her tracks on the stairs. "Ignore her."

Outside, they tore off their suits and jumped in the car.

"That comment was totally uncalled for."

"It was," Lorne agreed. "You've got to let comments like that go over your head. Christ, back in the day when I was dealing with the spiky Jacques Arnaud, there were times when I could have quite easily throttled the bloody man."

Sally sniggered. "And look how that turned out."

Lorne fell quiet, and Sally noticed her wipe away a sneaky tear that had slipped onto her cheek.

She patted Lorne's thigh and whispered an apology, "I didn't mean to upset you."

"You haven't, not really. He was a special man, at least he turned out to be, eventually. Maybe it's an unforgiving trait with all pathologists. What was Simon like when you had to deal with him professionally?"

Sally cast her mind back and nodded. "I have to admit, he had his moments."

"And how did you deal with his bouts of bloody-mindedness?"

"I brushed them aside. Heck, I still married the mardy sod, didn't I?"

Lorne laughed. "He's hardly mardy. I bet he was an angel compared to Jacques."

"Probably. Come on, let's get some caffeine and a sarnie down our necks, quick smart."

THEY FOUND a quaint little coffee shop in Acle and ordered a bacon roll and a flat white each. Halfway through their lunch, Sally's mobile rang. She glanced down to find Pauline's name filling the tiny screen. She completed her mouthful then answered it on the third ring.

"At last, I was just about to hang up."

"Sorry, I was in the ladies'."

"TMI. Can you come back to the house?"

"Why? Have you found something?" Sally wiped away the grease on her lips and gulped a mouthful of coffee.

"You really think I'd be calling you for a chat if I hadn't?"

"We'll be ten minutes, if that." Sally hung up and gobbled down half of her bacon roll and waited for Lorne to do the same.

"Umm... why are you rushing?" Lorne queried. "It's not like the body is going anywhere, is it?"

Sally flopped back in her seat and nodded. "That's true. Okay, let's finish this and then make a move. Hopefully Pauline will be too busy to notice if we're a few minutes late."

"Hey, if she says anything, tell her we got stuck behind a

tractor, there are plenty of those on the road at the moment, during harvest time."

"You tinker. I'll bear that in mind for whenever you're late for work."

"Er... yeah, I think I might have shot myself in the foot mentioning that one. Time to get my thinking cap on for another plausible excuse I can use in the future to appease my tyrant of a boss."

Sally sat upright, tore a piece off what was left of her roll and launched it at her partner. "Tyrant, my arse... I'll show you what a meanie I can be when pushed to my limits, young lady."

Lorne chewed her fingers. "Oh no, I'm terrified now."

"So you should be. Finish your lunch. That's an order."

WHEN THEY ARRIVED BACK at the house, they pulled on their third protective suit of the day.

"This is getting expensive and a little tedious," Sally grumbled.

"I hear you. Hopefully, the end result will be worth it."

"Come on, I'm eager to get inside and have a look."

They completed their ensemble with fresh booties over their shoes and attaching their masks.

"Job done! I feel like a Martian again."

"No comment," Lorne replied.

Sally's stomach muscles contracted as she climbed the stairs to the main bedroom. Pauline was over by the far wall. The team had clearly begun tearing the wall down in a different part of the room to where they'd been earlier. She turned when the floorboards creaked beneath them.

"Ah, you've finally made it."

"Sorry, you know what it's like at this time of the year. We got stuck behind a couple of tractors; they must have been on a farmers' day out."

"Ha, likely story. You're here, that's all that matters."

They walked further into the room.

Sally's gaze fixed on the patch in the wall that had been exposed, now that Pauline had taken a step to the side. "What the fuck?"

"Exactly. We knew we'd find something, so you needn't act shocked."

"There's thinking it and being confronted by the truth, and that's some truth sitting right there. Male or female?"

"Give me a bloody chance. I rang you as soon as we discovered the skeleton. I'm going to need to get it out of there first before I can determine what the gender is. I lived up to my end of the bargain and contacted you as soon as we found human remains."

"And I appreciate that, thank you."

"There's no need. It's what I would have done for any other SIO working the case."

Another slap in the face. Thanks, Pauline. You can get off your high horse now. Sally chose not to respond to the comment, avoiding further confrontation with the pathologist.

She and Lorne stood back while the team continued to tear out chunks of the wall and catalogue them. It was another two hours before Pauline finally gave the all-clear for the skeleton to be moved.

"Let's cover it and then move it. John, have you got all the photos you need, just in case the unthinkable happens?"

"All sorted, boss, don't worry," the tech replied. He placed his camera back in its case and returned to assist the rest of the team.

Sally watched on, her fingers tightly crossed at her side. "What if it falls apart when touched?"

"There's every chance it will. I'd be very surprised if it remained intact," Lorne said.

"Bugger. What then?"

"Don't worry, it's not worth speculating about, not until or unless it happens."

Sally's gaze remained focused on the skeleton. She didn't have a clue herself if the victim was male or female, but her heart went out to the person as she considered how they had got there in the first place. Foul means had to be at the top of the agenda. "Horrible. How could someone bury another person in a bloody wall?"

"It takes all sorts to make up this world of ours. Nothing should surprise us any more, you know that as well as I do."

"Still hard to believe. Do you think this Ronald did it, you know, after he inherited the house?"

"You're going to need to hold fire on the speculation until Pauline can give us her expert opinion on how long the person has been deceased."

"In your experience, is the body preserved when put in a wall or not?"

Lorne shrugged. "Unlikely. Again, I'm no expert, not really. The bodies we discovered at that house in London were mostly buried either in the concrete or stored in the attic. Attics are warm places, so the skeletons we uncovered up there had deteriorated far more than those found in the concrete. Like I said, it really depends on the circumstances. Every case needs to be assessed individually."

Sally nodded. "I understand. Can you imagine killing someone and even considering putting them behind a wall? Surely the killer would have known the remains would have been discovered soon enough?"

"Most killers don't think things through clearly, do they? They'll dispose of the body as they see fit."

They watched on in silence as the four members of the

tech team covered the skeleton and began the process of trying to remove it from its resting place. Several seconds later, the operation came to a halt when a bone clunked on the bedroom floor.

"Careful. Take your time, there's no rush," Pauline advised her team.

The techs agreed and shifted their footing to maintain a better stance while they started again.

"Your left, John. That's it. Now, Eric, you move the upper half to the right," Pauline instructed. She stood back and studied the angles and then ordered, "You're almost there. One more inch towards you, John, and the shoulder should be clear. If this doesn't work, we're going to need to have a rethink, maybe demolish some more of the wall."

In the end, there was no need to stop the operation again as the skeleton was now fully dislodged and free of its confines. The remains were gently placed on a plastic sheet the team had laid out on the floor behind them.

"Can we have a closer look?" Sally asked, once she felt everyone had got their breath back and the tension had eased slightly.

Pauline beckoned her and Lorne to come closer, and the cover was removed from the remains. Pauline got down on her haunches and studied the hip bones. Within minutes, she was back on her feet and took a step towards Sally.

"Female. Don't start bombarding me with questions, that's all I can give you at this stage."

"Fair enough. That narrows it down a bit."

"Hang on, boss, I can see something else behind the wall," John called over. He was on bended knee close to the opening with his torch lit.

Pauline shot across the room and peered into the gap. "We need to remove whatever it is, carefully. Any ideas what we're dealing with, John?"

"Something glinting down there. I'm guessing it's jewellery of some kind."

Sally approached but gave them enough breathing space to carry out their work unhindered. "That's great, it could make the identification process much easier for us."

"Absolutely. Okay, John, I'll hold the torch, you get in there if you can. If you're struggling, we'll have to consider taking down the lower part of the wall."

"I'll give it a go first, boss."

Pauline stood to one side, allowing him better access to the opening in the plasterboard once he'd repositioned himself. His bone cracked, and he winced as he contorted himself into an awkward position.

"I think it's going to be just out of reach."

"Do your best."

John twisted further and inched his way closer to the wall. Eventually, he raised his other hand in a sign of triumph. One of the other techs had an evidence bag at the ready and sprang forward to give it to him.

"Hold it open and I'll drop it in."

John placed the items in the bag and got to his feet, dusted his suit down and took the bag from his colleague.

Sally and Lorne inched forward and stood next to Pauline who asked, "What is it, John?"

"They need a good clean. I'm surmising it's a wedding ring and possibly a locket."

Eric collected something from his kit bag and handed it to John.

"Thanks." John took the brush and with his gloved hand reached into the bag for the first item. It turned out to be a wedding ring with an inscription inside.

"Can you read it?" Sally asked.

"*A, love you now and forever, T.*"

"It's a start," Sally replied, keen to see what the locket held inside, if anything.

The locket proved difficult for John to open wearing his gloves.

Getting frustrated, Pauline handed him a scalpel. "Here, try this."

Initially, John's hand shook, but eventually, he sucked in a breath, and the catch sprang open to reveal two photos, one of a man in his mid-to-late thirties and the other was of two children, a boy and a girl, one possibly seven or eight and the other maybe ten or eleven.

"Excellent, it's obviously her family. That should narrow the search down for us. Do you need us to be here any longer?" Sally faced Pauline and asked.

"No, it's time for you to get on with the investigation. Let me know what you find ASAP."

"We will. Thanks, and er... I apologise about earlier," Sally muttered.

"It's forgotten about. Now scram, let us get on with our work."

CHAPTER 4

 *ack in 2018*

TIM HAD RECEIVED numerous phone calls from the kidnapper during the day. The person had asked several questions about how the production was going and also made a point of telling Tim not to contact the police.

Shocked, Tim had sat in his office, his hand reaching for the phone every now and then. *Should I ring the police? I've failed my family, yet again. Why am I not thinking straight about this?* He kicked himself under the table, catching his ankle with the heel of his other shoe. Pain came but instantly diminished. He'd let his family down and now he couldn't see any way of getting them out of the situation, not unless he sought outside help.

He buried his head in his hands, his mind swirling like a tornado until what he considered a possible solution popped into his head. He rang Patrick, a friend from university, for help.

"Pat, hi. It's Tim Farrant, have you got a minute for a chat?"

"Hello, Tim. Long time no see or hear. How's it going?"

"Okay. I'm in desperate need of assistance and I can only think of you to get me out of the jam I'm in, through no fault of my own, I hasten to add."

"Go on, you've got me intrigued. What's up? If I can help, you know I will."

"It's… well… it's a difficult one, mate. I'm going to need to ask you to keep this information to yourself for now."

"I'm listening. Should I take a seat? It sounds serious."

"It is. It could be deadly serious." *God, why did I have to utter that word? Damn, now I can't think straight. I'm going to get tongue-tied.* He contemplated ending the call, but then an image of Amanda and the kids swam into his sore head. "It's a bit of a tricky situation."

"What is? Come on, Tim, you're worrying me now. Spit it out."

"I'm trying to, believe me. This is the toughest of days for me, and I really can't see an end in sight, not from where I'm sitting."

"What's that supposed to mean? Tim, you're going to have to get a move on, I've got a dentist appointment in thirty minutes."

"Sorry, no, you deal with that first and ring me back later."

"No way. You're obviously upset about something, tell me."

He closed his eyes and let the words seep out in a whisper. "Amanda and the kids have been kidnapped."

"What did you frigging say? Speak up, I could have sworn you said your family had been kidnapped. Please, tell me I misheard you."

"You didn't. I don't know what to do. I should be on cloud

nine here, having developed a new line of chocolate bars to get out there on the market and, here I am, sitting in my office absolutely bricking it. Wondering how I can get us all out of this ruddy mess."

"Jesus, I'm coming over. We shouldn't discuss this over the phone. I'll be ten to fifteen minutes max, hang in there."

"No, wait, what about your appointment?" Tim asked, suddenly panic-stricken at having to come face to face with a friend he hadn't been in touch with for at least five years.

"I'll postpone it. This can't wait, it's an emergency, man. We need to rescue your family, and quickly, before..."

"No, don't go there. Okay, you know where the factory is, don't you?"

"I do. I'll see you soon."

Tim hung up and left his desk. He peered out of the huge window overlooking the older production line, instantly regretting his office didn't have a view of the new one. But that shouldn't matter, not now, he had far more important things to consider.

His secretary knocked on the door around ten minutes later and announced Pat's arrival.

"Send him in, Thelma, thanks."

Pat entered the room, but to Tim's amazement, he wasn't alone. With him was a man in a blue suit and red tie, who must have been in his forties, judging by the signs of grey showing at his temple.

"Hi, Tim, it's good to see you." Pat shook his hand enthusiastically.

"Thanks for coming, Pat. Who's this?"

"Ah, this is a good friend of mine, DI Bob Addis. I brought him along to lend a hand."

"What? No. He has to leave. The kidnappers warned me what would happen to my family if I got the police involved."

"Why don't we all calm down and take a seat?" Addis said.

58

He gestured at the chairs around the conference table on the far side of the room. "Shall we sit here?"

Tim closed his eyes, doing his best to steady his racing heart. He opened them again to see Pat and DI Addis already seated at the table, waiting for him to join them. Addis had his notebook and pen at the ready.

"This is going against my better judgement. If this backfires, where will that leave me?"

"It won't," Addis assured him. "Take a seat and tell us how this all came about."

Tim reluctantly sat between the two men. He wasn't sure if he should feel angry or grateful to Pat for bringing Addis to the factory. He supposed only time would tell. He sat and clenched his hands together in front of him. "I've been receiving these strange calls for months. To begin with, I thought they were hoax calls, possibly from a competitor who had got wind of the fact that we had a new line about to go into production, so I basically ignored them. Then, as soon as the line started up and the new chocolates began to roll out, I received a call from this person telling me that he was holding my wife and children hostage."

"Did you receive any proof of that?" Addis glanced up from his notes and asked.

"Yes, I spoke to Amanda. She sounded terrified, and who could blame her? She screamed, then my kids shouted. The kidnappers hurt my son while I was on the phone. Who knows what will happen if they find out that I've gone running to the police?"

"You said kidnappers. How do you know there are more than one?" Addis asked the most obvious of questions.

"Amanda told me. Asked me if I knew what they wanted from me."

"Ah, okay. And have the kidnappers contacted you since this morning?"

"Yes, it's very strange. I've received several calls from them during the day. I'm a nervous wreck. I flinch every time the phone rings."

"Of course you do, that's to be expected," Pat said. "Don't worry, Tim, Bob will take the matter in hand and have your family back with you in no time at all, won't you, Bob?"

"I can't promise that, Pat. Let's try not to get ahead of ourselves here."

"What? Then why are you here? I thought you were going to help?" Tim asked. "I wouldn't have revealed my predicament if I thought you were thinking of toying with me. I'm at my wits' end, I can't imagine my life without my family."

"Okay, I'll see what I can do. We're going to need to hear all the facts before I can begin the investigation."

"That is all the facts. There's nothing more to tell."

"Can I see your phone?"

Tim went back to the desk, collected his mobile and gave it to Addis. "It's a waste of time, the number was withheld."

"That's unfortunate and will put a spanner in the works."

Tim retook his seat. "Are you telling me you won't be able to trace the number?"

"That's correct."

"Again, why are you here? What experience do you have?"

"Twenty years in the Force."

"Jesus, I meant dealing with kidnappers?" Tim said, his frustration by now evident in his tone.

"None. There won't be a lot of officers in the Force who will have. This isn't the States. Out there they have trained negotiators on the payroll."

"And you reckon telling me that is going to reassure me? Are you insane?"

Addis slammed his notebook shut and glanced at Pat. "I'm inclined to agree with Tim, this clearly isn't going to work out. I'm sensing that your friend is doubting my ability as a copper. There's little I can do to alter that, if the trust is missing in the first place."

"No, Bob, please, we can't desert him. Think of his wife and kids and the situation they're in through no fault of their own."

Addis sighed. "I am. Believe me, I came here with good intentions, but it's obvious to me that Tim isn't in the least bit interested in working with me, are you?"

Addis faced Tim, searching for an answer.

Tim's shoulders slouched in defeat. "I'm sorry. I'm confused. I have the kidnappers' warning replaying over and over in my head, you know, telling me what would happen if I got the police involved, and here you are. How would you be reacting if the tables were turned?"

"While I can understand what you're saying, I need to also point out that I'm not the enemy here. I've dropped in as a favour to Pat. It's entirely up to you if you want my help or not."

Tim's gaze dropped to his hands, and he wrung them together, unsure how to respond. He wanted his wife and children back, of course he did, but what would happen if he went against the kidnappers' wishes and brought the police in? He could only envisage it ending one way... badly. Eventually, he made the bold move and said, "I'm going to have to decline your offer. And if my reasons aren't obvious then there's very little I can say or do to change that."

Addis pushed back his chair and tucked his notebook into his pocket. "Then I must declare this meeting over. I have people out there, the general public, genuinely in need of my help. Wishing you every success in getting your family back, it sounds like you're going to need it." He strode, heavy-footed, towards the door.

Tim's gaze shot between Pat's shocked expression and

Addis's retreating back until Addis reached the door of the office.

"No. Stop! Don't run out on me. Not when I'm so desperate."

Addis stopped and slowly turned on his heel. "Are you sure about this?"

Tim didn't get the chance to answer because his mobile rang. The three of them stared at each other.

"Yes, I'm sure," Tim felt obliged to say when he saw that the number was a withheld one.

Addis dashed back to the table. "Very well. Answer the call, put it on speaker. We won't say a word, will we, Pat?"

A shocked-looking Pat shook his head vigorously. "No, I promise. Good luck."

Addis raised a warning finger. "Act naturally, by that I mean, act the way you always do when you're dealing with the kidnapper. If you don't, he'll suspect something is wrong."

Tim nodded, and his hand trembled as he answered the phone and immediately pressed the speaker button. "Hello, Tim Farrant. How can I—"

"Help you?" the kidnapper finished off his sentence and laughed.

"Oh, it's you. I was expecting another call from a supplier."

"Bullshit. But then, we both know you're a first-grade bullshitter, don't we?"

"I'm not… it happens to be the truth."

"Name the supplier?"

Tim's mind went blank. Addis desperately searched over his shoulder and scribbled the name *Lockyer* on his notebook after spotting something on a bookshelf close by.

"Lockyer," Tim shouted.

Addis winced and closed his eyes.

"What's wrong, Timmy boy, you sound mighty jumpy to me. Has something happened at that end?"

"No, everything is fine. Wouldn't you be jumpy if your wife and children were being held hostage?"

"Ah, you have a valid point, I'll give you that one." The kidnapper laughed a second time. "And how's the production of the new line coming along? Still flying out, is it, on the back of the lorries yet?"

"Yes, it's all good. Lorries are being loaded as we speak, and two are out on the road already."

"Good, good. All that hard work must be a relief for you after months and months of planning, eh?"

"Yes. It's been a constant source of frustration over the last few months, but with everything running as smooth as clockwork now it's a great relief."

"I'm glad you're relieved. Shame you're still eager to put your business before your family."

His wife screamed in the background, then his daughter and finally his son. Tears misted Tim's eyes. Addis raised his hand, warning him to remain calm.

"Please, you've got this all wrong. The business means nothing to me compared to them. Won't you let them go?"

"Not going to happen. And stop fooling yourself into believing you're saying all the right things. All you're doing is getting yourself deeper in the shit."

"How am I? I'm telling you the truth, responding to your questions the only way I know how, truthfully."

"Like fuck. I've told you before, you can't kid a kidder, Timmy boy. Who are the two men sitting in the office with you?"

Tim's eyes widened, and he slapped a hand over his mouth. Panic-stricken, he stared at Addis. Regaining his composure, and keeping his voice level, he replied, "What two men? I don't know what you're talking about."

The kidnapper went silent on them, but the screams of his family ripped at his heart.

"No, no, don't hurt them. They've done nothing wrong."

"Ah, but you have. You went back on your word, and now they're going to be the ones who suffer the consequences."

The line went dead.

Tim flopped his head onto his outstretched arms on the desk. "What have I done?"

Addis ensured the line was closed on Tim's mobile and placed a hand on his shoulder. "You mustn't blame yourself."

Tim bolted upright and stared straight ahead of him at the glass wall, overlooking his factory floor. "Who else am I going to blame? He knows the police are involved now; my family are fucking doomed. I might as well jump through that fucking window and end it all. I'm nothing without them, absolutely fucking nothing."

Pat reached over and grasped his arm, but Tim shrugged him off.

"Why did you have to bring him here? I trusted you. Now, between us, we've put my family in further jeopardy that could eventually lead to them losing their lives."

"Sorry, chum," Pat said, sounding choked. "If I'd known it would lead to this, I would never have brought Bob here today. I'm gutted for you."

Too stunned to speak, Tim sat there and rocked back and forth in his chair. His family's screams reverberating through his head.

"Tim, you need to get a grip. Crumbling into pieces at this stage isn't going to be the answer to this problem. We need to come up with a viable proposition that will eventually bring your family back home to you."

Tim shook his head. "It's too late for that. He must have eyes on the factory to know you're here."

"Possibly. Or, have you considered the kidnapper has someone on the inside, feeding him information?"

Tim's shock rose to yet another level. "There's no way. I'm surrounded by hand-picked staff who I can rely on. You're talking out of your arse if you believe that."

"Am I? Didn't you tell us the first call came in this morning, as soon as the production line started up? Or am I mistaken?"

Tim cast his mind back to the start of the day. "Oh my God, you're right. Shit. Every man and his dog were invited to go down there and take a look, including all the office staff. So, if I do have a traitor in the ranks, it could be any one of them and I'd be none the wiser. I'm inclined to believe they have someone on the outside, possibly hidden in the grounds, keeping an eye on the factory and reporting back to the man in charge."

Addis paused to contemplate Tim's statement. "Possibly. What do you want to do? Are you willing to keep me on board, or do you want me to jump ship now?"

"Before the kidnapper rang, I was willing to work with you, but now, I can't take the risk. I'm going to have to do this alone."

Addis shook his head. "I think you're doing the wrong thing, but it's your call."

All Tim could think about was the pain and torture his family was going through at the hands of the kidnappers. "I can't. No, I won't do it. I have to deal with them on my own."

"Fair enough. Then we'll leave you to it. I'll give you my card, should you have a change of mind. One more thing I think you need to consider before I leave."

Tim frowned and asked, "What's that?"

"What are the kidnappers after? Have they made any demands yet?"

"Initially they told me not to start up the production line, then that all changed, and they urged me to get the boxes loaded and out for delivery, but they've said nothing since. That's why I'm so confused about all of this. Nothing appears to be straightforward, and the kidnappers seem to be doing their best to keep me tied up in knots."

"Something doesn't sit right about that," Pat chipped in. "Sorry if you believe I've caused you any extra stress or trouble bringing Bob here today, Tim, I genuinely believed I was doing the right thing. Having listened to what the kidnapper has to say, I'm at a loss what to suggest you should do next."

Pat left his seat and slapped Tim on the shoulder, then he and Addis walked towards the door.

"There's nothing left for either of us to say, Tim." Addis turned and said, "Give me a call if you decide you could do with my help in the future. Good luck. Keep your wits about you. It's the only way you and your family are going to get through this traumatic ordeal."

"Thanks for the advice. I hope I haven't offended you, turning down your attempts to assist me. Hopefully you'll understand my need to go along with the kidnappers' instructions. I couldn't live with myself if anything... that's the wrong thing to say, let's try, if anything *further* happened to my family."

"We get that," Pat said. "Ring me if you need any advice or want to vent."

"I will. Thanks, guys. For coming here today and offering me your support. I hope my decision doesn't come back to haunt me."

The two men nodded and left his office.

Tim remained seated, staring at the rear wall, his thoughts lying with his wife and kids. *Please, God, I'm not a religious man as you know, but please keep them safe and out of harm's way.*

His mobile rang, pulling him out of his reverie.

"Tim, Tim, Tim. Whatever have you done?"

"I'm sorry. Don't punish my family for my mistakes."

"It's too late."

The line went quiet. Tim expected to hear his family's screams in the background. Instead, there was nothing.

"What can you hear, Timmy boy?"

After a lengthy pause, he swallowed down the acid burning his throat and replied, "Nothing. Please, tell me you haven't..."

"Haven't what? Go on, say the words."

"Ki... lled th... em," Tim mumbled, the words catching in his throat for a moment or two before he released them.

"Not yet. We're biding our time, though. The ball, as they say, is in your court, Timmy."

"Tell me what you want, and I'll give it to you, providing you release my family."

The kidnapper laughed, high-pitched, bordering on hysterical. "You really think you're in a position to make demands? Is that what the copper is telling you? He's wrong. I know he's left the building. Is that a good or bad thing?"

"You have to believe me, I didn't involve the police, I swear I didn't. I reached out and asked my friend, Pat, for advice, and he dropped by and brought the copper with him. They've gone now, I promise, I have no intention of involving them in this. You made it perfectly clear what would happen if I rang them... I didn't."

"And you expect me to believe you?"

"Yes, because it's the truth."

"We'll see. As you've probably cottoned on by now, I have my spies everywhere. You'd be wise to remember that and keep that information uppermost in your mind when dealing with me. Am I making myself clear?"

"Yes. Tell me what you want, and I'll give it to you."

"I mean it, one false move on your part, and either your wife or one of the kids will find out how sharp the knife being held to their throats is."

"No, please. Don't do anything rash. I'm willing to listen to your demands. Tell me what they are."

Another long, drawn-out silence was followed by the kidnapper whistling down the line. "Let's see now. Okay, why don't we put all our cards on the table?"

Tim waited, his muscles anxiously clenching and unclenching until his tormentor spoke again.

"We want... twenty million pounds... by the end of tomorrow. That gives you around thirty hours to get the money together."

"What? I can't come up with that kind of money, let alone within that timeframe. I don't have the funds to cover the ransom."

"In that case, I'll call back tomorrow, give you the chance to say farewell to your family. Get working on it. Their fate is in your hands."

The call ended. Tim froze on the spot and only pulled himself out of his dazed state when Thelma knocked on the door and poked her head into the room.

"Tim. Are you okay? I was going to make myself a drink and wondered if you wanted one."

"No, I need something stronger." He forced his wobbly legs to carry him back to his desk. He opened the bottom drawer and removed the bottle of scotch he kept there.

"If you're sure. I'll leave you to it. Give me a shout if you need anything."

"I will, don't worry. Actually, no, I won't be needing you for the rest of the day. Go home to your family. Make the most of them, you never know when you might lose them."

"Umm... is there something you're not telling me?"

"No, yes, I don't know any more. Just go home, Thelma."

"But I'm worried about you. I sense there's something you're keeping from me."

He threw his glass at the door, just missing her head. "I said get out!"

The door slammed behind his sniffling secretary. He regretted his actions and ran after her to apologise, only to see Thelma shooting through the outer office door. He stopped in his tracks, dropped to his knees and sobbed.

CHAPTER 5

$\mathcal{T}$he team gathered around, munching on the lunch Sally had bought them on the way back to the station, while she summed up what they had discovered about the house and its inhabitants so far.

"So, Ronald Edgar, the previous owner. What we need to find out is if he had any relatives or significant others who can fill in the gaps we have with the history. The caller this morning told me the body had been there for five years. The owner at the time was Nancy Hart. Did Nancy leave the property at all before her dementia set in? Did Ronald Edgar put the body behind the wall, or was it Nancy herself? Hard to imagine it being the latter, but I don't think it would be wise for us to dismiss anything at this early stage."

"And what about the victim?" Lorne asked when Sally paused.

"That should be simple enough, I hope. We'll search the Missing Persons' Database, see what shows up. Don't forget we've got the ring, or more importantly, the inscription on the ring to guide us, which hopefully will narrow the field down. Furthermore, we have the locket with the picture of her family, a partner and two children, at least I'm presuming they're of her family. Joanna, do you want to deal with that?"

"On it, boss." Joanna jotted down the details then took a bite out of the sandwich sitting on the desk beside her.

"Jordan, why don't you search the archives, going back five years? See if there were any major cases in the news around that time. What's bugging me is the fact the victim was deliberately buried behind that wall and not just dumped in the woods or in a lake, you know, the usual way we discover bodies in a cold case."

"I have to draw attention to the smell that must have emanated as the body decomposed," Lorne added.

Sally nodded. "It must have been horrendous, but if Nancy had dementia, we don't know how extreme it was. As we know, there are different levels of the disease. Would she have been able to detect the smell? Perhaps it became a smell that she was able to ignore, or one that she grew accustomed to after a while, the same with the carers. I fear that part of the puzzle is going to be difficult for us to ascertain."

THE TEAM ALL PULLED TOGETHER, and within three hours they had uncovered a few interesting details that Sally believed could prove vital to the investigation.

The one fact they had discovered, which wasn't going to help them, was that according to the solicitor they had tracked down in Devon, Ronald didn't have any relatives and the house was yet to be sorted as he died intestate, therefore, the house would be passed to the Crown. They were still waiting to dot the I's and cross the T's on that, the decision imminent.

"So, we can set that aside and stop wasting time on that aspect, maybe revisit it later if we get stumped," Sally said after Jordan delivered the disappointing news.

"Anything else you need me to research, boss?"

"I don't think so, not for now, Jordan. I'm sure there'll be more digging needed soon, there's bound to be." Sally stopped by Joanna's desk next and pulled up a chair. "Right, what nuggets of information have you managed to find from MissPers?"

"Well, after trawling through the database from twenty eighteen, I've come up with three possible names. The first is Amanda Farrant, the second is Alice Underhill, and the third and final one is Annabelle Kendal."

"Mind if I butt in here?" Lorne called across the room.

Sally swivelled in her seat to face her partner. "Of course not. Does one of those names mean anything to you, Lorne?"

"Yes, I've been going through the newspaper archives and came up with this." She pointed at her screen.

Sally patted Joanna on her hand and left her seat. "I shall return."

"No bother," Joanna replied.

Lorne reached for the chair tucked under the desk next to hers and dragged it closer for Sally to sit on.

"Thanks. What have you got?"

"This."

Lorne angled her screen so Sally had a bird's eye view of it.

After reading the headlines, Sally's jaw dropped open. "What the fuck! Hang on, I seem to remember hearing, or should I say reading, about this case at the time. There were all sorts of implications with it from what I can recall, but I can't for the life of me think of what they were. It'll come, I'm sure."

"It's just heartbreaking to think what this family went through. As if kidnapping wasn't enough..."

Sally sighed and expelled a further large breath. "Poor buggers. That would match up with the initials on the ring, and looking at the family photo, I recognise the faces from the locket as well. This is great news. Well done, team."

"Do you want me to try and find out where the family are now? I'm guessing they'll no longer be at the mansion in the article, not after the funds were used to pay the ransom."

"Yes, see what you can find out, Lorne. Do you need a hand? Jordan is free."

"I don't mind. One more thing, there's no mention of the wife at the end of this piece. The children, yes, but not the wife."

"I'll keep racking my brain, see if anything else comes to mind about the case. Does it mention who was in charge of the investigation?"

"I'll read through it thoroughly, see what I can find out, if Jordan can do some extra research on the family for me."

"I'm on my way," Jordan shouted.

Sally squeezed Lorne's shoulder. "Great job. If we can get this case wrapped up quickly, we might get to enjoy our weekend jaunt after all."

Lorne laughed. "Is that you doing your best to tempt fate again?"

Sally winced. "I hope not. A trip on the boat is just what I need right now." She returned to Joanna. "Lorne thinks she's found something but, just to keep our options open, can you look up each of the files for me? We're looking for up-to-date information for each of the families."

"I'll see what I can find, boss."

Sally went over to the whiteboard and entered the three possible names then put a circle around Amanda Farrant's. "Could it be you?" Sally whispered.

Twenty minutes later, she revisited Lorne and asked, "Anything yet?"

"I've got the name of the officer in charge of the case, DI Bob Addis, if that rings a bell?"

"It does, not sure why. I'll look into it and get back to you. What about an address for the husband, Jordan, anything yet?"

"Not yet, boss."

"Wait, he had a factory over near Acle," Lorne said. "What was it called?" She scrolled through the article again and struck lucky a few seconds later. "Here it is, Comfort Chocolates."

"Yummy, a chocolate factory. Might be worth us taking a trip out there if nothing shows up on the system. They might feel sorry for us and dish out some freebies."

"Wishful thinking on your part. Maybe years ago. I don't know any firm who gives away their products these days, not with the way things are in our economy."

"A girl can dream, can't she?" Sally grinned. "Come on, guys, I need an address for Farrant. Who's going to come up trumps first?"

The team got their heads down, and finally, twenty minutes later, it was Jordan who came up with a possible address for Timothy Farrant.

"Umm… I've got news on DI Addis as well," Lorne said.

Sally wandered across the room, sensing the news was bad.

"What's that?" Sally leaned over her partner's shoulder and whispered, "Shit! That's not good, is it?"

CHAPTER 6

 *ack in 2018*

TIM WOKE the following morning and studied himself in the mirror, loathing his pitiful reflection. Not just for the dishevelled mess he barely recognised, but peering deep into his eyes, he detested what he saw within their depths.

He'd only managed to grab a few hours' sleep, once his mind had calmed down and stopped working overtime. He tried to make a conscious effort not to think about the terror his family must be going through. Instead, he decided to focus on what he had to do to get them out of this mess, all of them.

Thankful that he'd had the foresight to have created an en suite in his office, it proved to be worth its weight in gold. He always kept a few changes of clothes in the small wardrobe he'd added, as well. Now he was reaping the benefits of what some had considered a crazy idea of his at the time.

Thelma arrived at five minutes to nine, later than usual,

but he didn't blame her, not after the way he'd treated her the day before. His first task for the day was to make amends. He wafted into her office as if he didn't have a care in the world, if only that were true, and sheepishly begged for her forgiveness.

"I don't know what came over me, Thelma. I hope you can find it in your heart to forgive me."

"I told Ken I wasn't going to come in today. You could have killed me yesterday if that glass had hit my head…"

"I doubt if that's true, but yes, it might have caused you a bad injury. Can we forget all about it and get on with our day?"

"As you've seen fit to apologise. I need to say one thing, though, Tim, before we start our day." She added a wagging finger and said, "If that ever happens again, I'm out of here. There'll be no talking me around next time."

"I promise to keep my temper in check going forward. It will never happen again, I assure you. I've never shouted at you before. Please regard the incident as a one-off."

Thelma mulled it over for a few moments and nodded. "That's true. Are you going to tell me what was wrong with you and why you've obviously spent the night in your office?"

"I'm not sure if I can put it into words yet. Can I get back to you later?"

Thelma shuffled the envelopes she'd collected from the post box outside on her way in and then glanced up at him. "It must be pretty bad to warrant that type of reaction. I'm here if you feel the need to have a chat."

"Thanks, maybe later. I'm going to be snowed under for a couple of hours. I haven't got any appointments pencilled in for today, have I?"

"No, I kept today clear, knowing that you'd probably

want to oversee what's going on with the new production line."

"Good thinking. Okay, I'll do my best to keep an eye on it, but there are numerous calls I need to make this morning."

"Let's start the day with a coffee, shall we? Have you eaten? I could pop next door to the baker's and buy you a couple of croissants."

"Sounds wonderful, you do look after me. Which is why I'm appalled at the way I treated you yesterday."

"It doesn't matter. I'm here if you need to chat, just remember that."

"I will." He smiled and left his secretary to get on with her chores.

Ten minutes later, he had a plateful of warm croissants and a steaming cup of rich roast coffee sitting on his desk. Thelma smiled and asked if he needed anything else.

"Nothing at this moment. Thanks for being so considerate and understanding, Thelma."

"I wish you'd tell me what is bothering you. A problem shared and all that."

The words entered his mouth and teetered on the tip of his tongue, but he swallowed them down with a sip of hot coffee that almost scalded his lips. "I can't. Maybe later, once I've made all the calls on my to-do list."

"I'll hold you to it. Give me a shout if you need a hand."

"I'll do that."

Thelma left him to eat his breakfast. He nibbled on a buttered croissant filled with strawberry jam and then pushed it aside, feeling guilty that his family were stuck somewhere, probably without any food or water in their stomachs. *How can I eat when I know they're starving? I just can't, it's not right.*

The aroma changed his mind a couple of minutes later. With

a clean plate, he picked up the phone and rang the bank to speak to the business manager who was on another call. His secretary told him she would get the manager to call Tim as soon as he was free. He waited and waited for the man to ring back. Nearly an hour later, his phone rang. He blew out the breath he'd sucked in when he realised who was on the other end.

"Hello, Mr Farrant. It's Clive Zanter here from Lloyds Bank. Sorry for the delay in getting back to you. The previous client's problem took longer than anticipated to sort out. What can I do for you today?"

"That's fine. Thanks for getting back to me. I have a simple request."

"Good, simple requests are always a bonus. What's yours?"

"I need a loan of twenty million pounds by tomorrow lunchtime."

Zanter laughed. "Oh, is that all? Yes, no problem, I can sign that off for you and have it in your account by the end of the day. How's that for service?" Zanter laughed.

"I'll hold you to it. I'm not joking, Clive. This is a genuine request."

"Oh, I see. Can I ask why you would need such a vast amount of money at short notice?"

"I can't tell you."

"Ah, then that's going to be a bit awkward. We would need some form of business plan and forecast from yourself before we can proceed."

"I can't supply one. This is a personal loan to me."

"Then I definitely won't be able to assist you, sir. I'm sorry."

Seething, Tim slammed down the phone and cursed for several moments under his breath. "What the fuck? How do people in my situation usually get funds to pay off a kidnapper?" He deliberated his predicament long and hard but was determined that he wouldn't give up at the first hiccup that got in his way. He called several more banks that morning. Only one of them was willing to lend a hand and even listen to his proposal. The others cut him off as soon as he mentioned the sum involved.

The young assistant promised to have a word with his manager and get back to him in a couple of hours.

"Thanks, I appreciate it. I'll keep my fingers crossed until I hear from you."

In the meantime, Tim distractedly tackled his post and a batch of emails that had arrived during the day. He hated being in limbo like this but had high hopes the young man at the last bank he'd tried wouldn't let him down.

Thelma knocked on the door soon after. She entered the room and closed it behind her. "Sorry to trouble you, Tim, I know how busy your morning is likely to be. I... umm... there's someone here to see you."

Tim frowned. "What's wrong, Thelma? You seem anxious."

"It's the Environmental Health Department, or should I say two of its officers out there, demanding to have a word with you."

"Oh my. Did they tell you what it was concerning?"

"No. I tried to get the information out of them, but they refused to speak to anyone other than the person in charge."

"Very well, in that case, you'd better show them in." Tim straightened his tie and shoved his plate and cup out of view on the floor beside him.

Thelma entered a few seconds later with two officious-looking young men in their thirties. Tim left his desk and came round to greet the men with an extended hand that they declined to shake.

"Mr Farrant, sorry to interrupt you. I'm Will Rogers, and

this is my colleague, Andy Bartlett. All right if we take a seat?"

"Of course. Go right ahead." Tim gestured for the men to sit in the two vacant chairs and rolled his eyes at Thelma. "Sorry, can we get you a drink?"

"Not for us, but thanks for the offer."

Tim shrugged. Thelma left the office, and Tim returned to his seat. He picked up a pen to keep his anxiety in check during the conversation. He'd never had an impromptu visit from anyone from the EH Department before and he found the whole scenario quite intimidating on top of the other current unnerving situation he was dealing with.

"Right, perhaps you wouldn't mind telling me what your visit is about?" he asked.

"Unfortunately, I have to hand you this," Rogers said. He slid a notice across the desk.

"And what is this?" Tim asked, confused. He read the document, and his heart sank to a new low. "You're ordering me to halt the production line? Why?"

"It has come to our attention that certain products have caused members of the public to become ill."

"What? This must be some kind of sodding joke. What products?"

"Have you recently rolled out a new line?"

"Yes, that's right. What type of illness are we talking about?"

"Serious ones. We're talking possible cases of poisoning. Suffice it to say, several people have been admitted to hospital."

"Oh shit! In hospital? I can't believe what I'm hearing." Tim ran his hands through his hair and closed his eyes. *Could this fucking week get any worse?* Suddenly overwhelmed, he excused himself and bolted for the bathroom where he promptly vomited. He rinsed his mouth and splashed cold water over his face then dried it with the small hand towel. His cheeks lacked any colour. His insides churned like a meat grinder as he returned to his office. "Sorry about that, I must have had a dodgy curry last night."

"Always best to steer clear of takeaways in our experience. We've had to close down a number of them in the area recently, for poor hygiene standards."

"Goodness, how awful. Umm… I really don't know what to say about the cases you've brought up regarding my products. We've never had to deal with an issue of this nature before. It's come as a huge shock to me."

"How many years has the factory been running?"

"Ten or eleven. I've been here from the beginning, although several partners have come and gone in that time." He placed a hand to his cheek and shook his head. "But why are you closing us down?"

"It's the law. We need to carry out a thorough search of the premises. We'll be unable to do that with your staff hanging around. You're going to need to send them home, allowing our team to conduct their investigation."

"And how long is that likely to take?" With that, his mobile rang, *Number Withheld* displayed on the screen. Tim was caught with an impossible dilemma on his hands. Did he answer the call or choose to ignore it with the officers present?

"Feel free to answer it, if you want."

Tim hesitated too long, and the phone fell silent. "Problem solved. I'm sure they'll ring back if it was urgent. I have more important things to sort out. I take it everything has to grind to a halt today, is that right?"

"That's correct. Right away, without further ado, in fact."

"Oh my." Tim's mobile rang again. *Shit, it must be them. What should I do? Fuck, fuck, fuck!*

"Why don't you take your call? We can wait."

81

Tim leapt out of his seat and answered the call over-looking one of the production lines that was about to be shut down. "Hello, Tim Farrant."

"Timmy boy. How the dickens are you? Sleep well last night in the office, did you? Couch comfy, was it?"

"Well enough, thanks. What do you want?" Tim asked, eager to get the kidnapper off the line so he could get back to the EH officers, who were about to wreak havoc with his business.

"Come now, Tim, that's a poor way to speak to me. Oh, yes, you're probably keen to get back to the Environmental Health officers, aren't you?"

"What? You know..." The penny suddenly dropped, and his legs wobbled beneath him. He lowered his voice and sneered, "This is down to you, isn't it? First you wanted the production stopped and then you were adamant that the new line should get out there, on the road ASAP. What have you done?"

"You mean apart from kidnapping your family and ruining your business in a week? Ooo, I'll have to think about that for a second or two."

"You bastard!" Tim hissed.

"Now, now, Timmy boy, not in front of the officers." Laughter rippled down the line, and then the kidnapper hung up.

"Everything all right, Mr Farrant?" Rogers asked.

Bile rose in his throat, and he dashed to the bathroom to empty his stomach again. *Shit, shit, shit! What kind of mess am I in? Who the fuck is doing this to me? More to the point, why are they doing this to me?*

A knock sounded on the door, interrupting his thoughts. "Mr Farrant, is there anything we can do to help?"

"No. I'm fine. Or I will be in a minute. Sorry to hold you up."

"It's okay, as long as you're all right in there."

"I am, I won't be long." Again, he splashed his face with water and rinsed out his mouth, dried himself, and then returned to his office to confront the two officers a second time. "Where were we?" As soon as he'd unleashed the words his mobile rang.

The three of them stared at the phone.

"Please, if it's urgent, answer it. Would you rather we left you alone to speak to the person in private?" Rogers said.

"No, definitely not. You know what, I'm just going to let it ring. It's not fair to hold you up longer than is necessary."

"Very well. We're going to need to go downstairs and turn off the machines with you. There, you'll have to dismiss the staff until we give you the go-ahead to begin production again."

His heart thumping against his ribs, he asked, "And how long is that likely to be?"

"How long is that proverbial piece of string?"

"That long, eh?" Tim jested, doing his best to disguise just how upset and angry he was that these two officious buggers were about to close down his business.

"We'll try and make it as stress-free and as painless as possible," Rogers assured him.

"Thanks, I appreciate that, I think." Tim headed towards the door. "Shall we?" He deliberately left his phone behind. *I know I'm probably putting my family's life in further danger but... shit! I'm between the Devil and the deep blue sea here... drowning fast whichever way you look at it.*

"Mr Farrant?" Rogers said.

Tim shook his head to clear it of all the anxious questions gushing through his mind. "Sorry, what did you say?"

"I asked how many staff you have working here."

"Oh, right. Umm... around thirty at the last count,

including drivers and the cleaner. Therefore, you'll be making a lot of people unemployed."

"Not really our fault, as such, but I agree, it's an unfortunate predicament you and your staff find yourselves in at present."

Tim bit down on his tongue, keen to unleash a torrent of curse words, but refrained from doing so when he mentally took a step back and assessed where doing that would be likely to get him. He showed the gents down the sweeping metal staircase to the factory floor and crossed the room to the massive machine at the far end of the room. He hit the Emergency Stop button, and it ground to a halt. Dozens of faces glanced his way, frowning.

"What's going on, Mr Farrant?" one of the supervisors, Hazel, ran up to him and asked.

"We've got a problem, Hazel. I need to shut down the factory immediately."

"What? Why?" she shouted in a high-pitched tone.

"These men are from the Environmental Health, and they have reports that some of the products coming off the line have been contaminated. As a precaution, we need to shut down the factory until the issue has been resolved. If you can relay the message to the rest of the staff and get everyone off the premises immediately, that would be a load off my mind, Hazel."

"Christ, what type of contamination?"

Tim shook his head. "Less questions and more action, that's what I need from you right now." He turned on his heel and gestured for Rogers and Bartlett to follow him into the next room to where the new production line was situated. A lump appeared in Tim's throat as he flicked the switch to shut down his newest line. The line that was supposed to save everyone's job but had, instead destroyed the name of the company and signed everyone's P45 for them if it was proved the illness was because of his products. "I'm sorry, ladies. Can you leave the room immediately? Hazel will fill you in next door. Thanks for all your hard work over the last few days."

The four women sitting on either side of the conveyor belt looked totally bamboozled by what was happening. They weren't the only ones. Tim was struggling to get his mind around the situation as well. It was as if someone had switched his autopilot on and he was carrying out instructions without really considering the consequences.

It'll hit me where it hurts once these guys have left and the silence on the factory floor smacks me in the face, whenever that's likely to be.

"Right, that's both production lines shut down, anything else?" Tim asked.

"We'd like to have a brief wander around the rest of the factory, in particular the prep area and the packaging room, if that's okay?" Rogers said.

His colleague, Bartlett, had produced a clipboard and appeared to be checking off items on a list. Tim should have asked, but he had more important things on his mind as an image of Amanda and the kids sprang into his head.

Why did I ignore the kidnappers? Why didn't I bring my phone with me? For fuck's sake, my wife is right, maybe I am guilty of putting this place before them.

"I'm sorry, I need to dash back upstairs to fetch my phone. Just in case..." He left his unfinished sentence dangling.

"Of course," Rogers said with a taut smile. "But first, if you wouldn't mind taking us to the preparation area?"

"Right, it's this way, follow me if you will." He turned left and walked up a small corridor to a room at the rear. He pushed open the door, and something scurried across the floor in front of them. Realising what it was, Tim squeezed his eyes shut. He opened them again to find the big furry creature standing in the middle of the room, preening itself. "Jesus! I can't believe this," Tim mumbled, utterly devastated by the cruelty and the gravity of what was occurring.

"I think we've seen enough. Unfortunately, this has given us the power to enforce an indefinite closure of these facilities, Mr Farrant."

"I don't know where that's come from. I know you're going to find this hard to believe when the evidence is staring us in the face, but I haven't got a clue how that frigging critter has gained access to this facility. I've never seen one on these premises before, I swear I haven't. Not that it's going to make any difference in your eyes. Someone is doing their best to sabotage my company."

"If that's what you truly believe, then you need to inform the police straight away," Rogers said, his gaze fixed on the huge critter acting as though it didn't have a care in the world.

"I can't. It's a delicate and complicated situation. Please don't ask me to reveal what I know. The damage has been done now. Just do what you have to do and let me get on with sorting this mess out. I'm going to need to ring my solicitor ASAP. Maybe he'll be able to tell me where I stand in all of this."

"I think that's the wisest thing you've said so far. I'm sorry you're being put through the mill like this. We carried out an investigation into previous reports on the factory before we showed up here today and found nothing, so we were surprised to hear about the incidents that have put these people in hospital. I'm sorry if you believe someone who may have some kind of grudge against you is doing this intentionally."

"They are, but I refuse to buckle under the stress. There's something far more sinister going on in my life at present; all of this is just the tip of the iceberg. Let's just say I totally get what the passengers on the *Titanic* went through on its maiden voyage."

"Look, my advice would be to give the police a call at your earliest convenience. If you do, it'll work in your favour during our enquiry."

Tim shook his head. "I can't do that. This is bigger than all of us put together. I'm in a kind of vortex, whirling round and round, spinning out of control, and I don't know where it's all going to end." His legs momentarily gave way beneath him, and he clung to the worktop next to him to steady himself.

"I can't pretend to know what that is supposed to mean. But we have to carry out the job we're paid to do and shut the factory down."

"I know that. I'm not trying to persuade you to do other-wise, I'm just... well, pleading with you to take everything into consideration when you make your decision as to whether you give the go-ahead to restart production or not."

"We'll consider all the facts, but the decision will be out of our hands."

"What do you mean?" Tim asked, his brow furrowing.

"It all boils down to what happens to the poor people who have been admitted to hospital, whether they make a full recovery or not."

Tim placed his hands over his face for a moment or two, giving himself time to think. Releasing his hands, he said, "I can't keep apologising, but believe me when I say that I never wanted any of this to happen. I'm just as distraught about the circumstances as the families are, more so. I can't hang around here, arguing the toss about the rights and wrongs of your procedures, I need to get on to my solicitor, now."

"At the end of the day, we're just carrying out our job

after some very serious allegations have come to our attention."

"I know," Tim said and marched out of the room, leaving Rogers and Bartlett to deal with the furry critter that had probably just put the final nail in his coffin.

He ran back through the factory, the staff trying to prevent him from leaving, bombarding him with dozens of questions, but he managed to dodge around them. He needed to put things into action right away if he was going to save his factory and, more importantly, his family.

I'm a selfish prick, still putting the factory before Amanda and the kids! When am I going to learn right from wrong? When it's too late, that's when.

Thelma leapt out of her seat the second he entered her office. "My God, I had no idea they possessed the powers to do such a thing. How long is the factory likely to be shut for, Tim?"

"I don't know. You might as well pack up and go home for the day, Thelma. I have some very important phone calls to make."

"I don't mind hanging around to help out, it's not like I have anything better to do. Why don't I get you a fresh cup of coffee? That'll help to put things right, for now at least."

"I don't want anything. Just go," he snapped.

Thelma reeled back, shocked by the ferociousness of his words. "I... was... it doesn't matter. I'll get my bag and go. Perhaps you'll ring me when you know what's going on with the business."

"Of course. I'm sorry, not for the way I just spoke to you, but for everything. In truth, I don't know when, or even if, the factory will ever open again. I wouldn't blame you if you started searching for another job."

"Surely it won't come to that, Tim. Nothing can be that bad, can it?"

"People are seriously ill in hospital. I'd say it's as bad as it can get, Thelma. I need to get on. Please don't interrupt me."

"I won't. Okay, I'll go. Would it be all right if I give you a call later, just to see how you're bearing up under the strain?"

Tim forced out a weak smile. "That's kind of you, thank you."

"It's the least I can do, although I'm willing to do more for you, if you need me to."

"I don't," he snapped again. "I need to press on. Take care, Thelma, and if I don't see you again, thanks for everything you've done for me in the past."

"I hope it won't come to us bidding farewell to each other. You know where I am if you need me."

"I do. Thanks."

He walked into his office and closed the door behind him. He spotted his mobile vibrating across his desk, and his heart sank for the umpteenth time that day. He hesitated before he finally picked up the phone. "Hello."

"How to piss me off and endanger the lives of your family members in one fell swoop."

"I'm sorry. I had the men from the EH to deal with, the ones you sent my way. I can't be expected to drop everything, not when my company is in jeopardy."

"A strange way of considering the plight you are in. What about your family, don't they count?"

"Of course they do. Forget I said anything. You've achieved your aim; the production lines have been closed down now."

"Partially achieved our aim. We still have the matter of twenty million smackeroos to consider."

"Jesus, talk about heaping the pressure on me. I'm doing my best to get the funds together, but you're not making it easy, sending the EH my way."

"I didn't. You brought that on yourself by rolling out that

new line that you were advised to abandon. All of this is down to your stubbornness at the end of the day, mate."

"Don't call me mate, I'm no mate of yours. Where are my wife and children? Are they safe?"

"For now. But I have to remind you, Timmy boy, that time is running out faster than you think."

"I know I've got a time limit to adhere to. You throwing this huge spanner in the works hasn't bloody helped. I don't know how you expect me to get those kinds of funds together during a normal working day, let alone one fraught with difficulties of this magnitude."

"Shit happens as they say. Get your act together and prove to me and your family how much they mean to you. Because from where I'm standing, you're bloody failing miserably."

"And who's fault is that?"

"Not mine, I can assure you. Come on, Tim, get into the groove. Like I've said already, time is running out for all of you."

"But…"

His response was interrupted by Amanda pleading with him. "Please, get us out of this mess, Tim, get them the money. There's no telling what they're going to do with us otherwise."

His wife was silenced with a slap, and she responded with a spine-tingling scream.

"Shit, don't hurt her, please, don't hurt any of them. I'm doing my utmost to get you that money. You're going to have to give me more time."

"Bollocks. You've got a deadline to meet. A minute over, and one of them dies."

The kidnapper hung up on him.

Tim flopped into his chair, feeling every bit defeated, the way he suspected the kidnapper wanted him to feel. He held his head in his hands while he tried to come up with a solution. So far, he'd only managed to cobble together around ten million, nowhere near enough to appease the kidnappers and get them to release his family.

The phone on his desk rang. Thelma must have switched them over before she'd left for the day. He answered it. "Tim Farrant, how can I help?"

"What the bloody hell is going on over there?" Barbara shouted.

"Hi, umm… well, there's nothing I can do about the Environmental Health bods coming in here and closing the factory down."

"What do you mean by that statement? You're the one running the fucking place. What's going on?"

Tim revealed what the EH officers had told him when they'd first arrived on site.

"What? Why are these people in hospital? How does something like this happen? I demand to know!"

"Some kind of poison, they believe, but they're awaiting the results from the tests they've run. It seems it has to do with the new line we introduced."

"What the fuck? Has anything like this ever happened at the factory before?"

"No, never. This is the first time EH have ever had an issue with the way we run things around here."

"And what about the rats?"

"What? How the heck do you know about that?"

"It doesn't matter. How the dickens did they get in the building? And why am I only just hearing about a rat infestation now?"

"Because it's the first I've heard about it, well, all of ten minutes ago. I repeat, who told you there was an issue here?"

"And I refuse to tell you. What, you seriously think I

would sink millions into a factory I didn't know the ins and outs of? You're an imbecile if you believe that."

"So, what you're effectively telling me is that you have a spy on the premises, right?"

"I wouldn't necessarily class them as a spy."

Tim paused to mull over the implications of what his partner was saying.

And the kidnappers know what's going on around here, too! A mere coincidence, or is there more to Barbara than meets the eye? A sleeping partner who has proved anything but in the last few days. My business went to pot the second she came on board, and my family have been kidnapped. What the fuck? Where has this twenty mill figure come from? Is all this about Barbara forcing my hand, trying to get the money back she invested in the company?

"Tim? Tim, are you still there?"

"I'm here. I have a lot to contemplate at present. I'm going to end this call before I say something derogatory that might ruin our working relationship before it has had a chance to get off the ground."

"What the hell does that mean? Don't you dare hang up—"

Too late. He paced the office, needing to calm down before he got his begging bowl out again. His landline rang. He ignored it, presuming it was probably Barbara trying to contact him.

Eventually, he stood there, silence all around him, leaving him to ponder how deep the shit surrounding him was. He had a tough time shifting the underlying feeling that all this had culminated since Barbara had come into his life. He did the only thing he felt was left open to him, he gave his former partner a call.

"Matt, how's it diddling?"

"Tim? Hey, it's great to hear from you. I thought I was in your bad books."

His former partner laughed, and Tim ground his teeth.

"Nah, all forgotten about now. Umm... this is just a quick one. What do you know about Barbara?"

"Hang on, yeah, I'll have another piña colada, thanks. Sorry, Tim, needs must while topping up my tan in the Caribbean."

"Lucky you. I'm in all kinds of disarray here." He cringed, regretting opening his big mouth and dropping himself in it.

"Overworked and underpaid, are you?" Matt jested, adding to his anger.

"Not exactly. You know as well as I do how that works out. A few gripes with the new owner, I mean, it's nothing I can't handle. I wanted to touch base to get a bit of background information on Barbara. So, what can you tell me?"

"Not much. I advertised the partnership on a website, and she got in touch with me virtually straight away. What's the problem, man?"

"A bloody website? Did you carry out any background checks on the woman first before you thought about taking her money and doing a bloody runner, leaving me neck-deep in the fucking shit?"

"Wait, what are you trying to say? That I didn't give two hoots about the company?"

"Fucking hell, where are you getting that idea from? Of course you frigging didn't. All you cared about was selling up so you could jump on a plane and start sunning yourself. Go on, tell me I'm wrong."

"Er... I'm not sure if you've lost the plot or what, Tim, but I don't have to lie here and take this crap from you. I ditched the company, there's no come back on me if you aren't getting on with your new partner. These things don't happen overnight. You're going to have to relax and take time to get to know her. Anyway, she signed up to be a silent partner. If she's not living up to her status, then slap her down."

"Fuck me. You have no idea the trouble you've caused."

"I've caused? Get a life and give me a break. I left you running a viable, profitable company. If you and that new partner of yours can't get along, how's that my problem?"

"For your information, the company has ground to a halt."

"What? Why?"

"I don't want to go into details now, but all this has raised my suspicions about Barbara."

Matt sighed. "Sorry, pal, I can't help you. I feel bad about the position you're in, but it has nothing to do with me. It was time for me to move on and start enjoying life."

"I wish you had run things past me first, given me time to sort something out that wouldn't have proved disastrous to the business."

"I regret not speaking to you, what more can I say, Tim?"

He felt like banging his head against the desk. "It's okay, what's done is done. Enjoy your retirement, Matt." He decided against burdening his former partner with his family's plight. The less people who knew about that travesty the better.

"Speak soon. Ring me if I can be of any help in the future, Tim, well... within reason, of course."

"Ha, if you've got twenty million lying around, that would come in handy about now."

"I haven't. Is that how much the factory is going to take to fix? Has one of the machines gone kaput? Is that what you're hinting at?"

"No, it's okay. Just ignore me. I'm sitting here feeling sorry for myself, that's all. I'll be right in a couple of hours. Have a nice life."

"Will do."

Tim jabbed his finger to end the call and tipped back in his chair. His gaze took in the moulding around the ceiling;

he'd never noticed that before. What a time to take in his surroundings. But what else was he to do when everything he'd worked for had bitten the dust? A knock on the door brought him back down to earth with a bang. He shot out of his chair and opened the door to find Rogers and Bartlett standing there.

"Come in, gents."

"We're going now. We've ensured there are no members of staff left on the premises and we're happy to take your word that production has ground to a halt. We'll report our findings to our boss and be in touch with you in the next few days about what to do to rectify the situation."

"I'll look forward to hearing your suggestions, because at the moment, I'm struggling to even think straight, let alone put all the wrongs right to this multi-million-pound company. I've got problems coming at me from every angle, but hey, you don't want to hear about that, you've done the deed and ruined my business within twenty minutes of setting foot inside my office."

He could tell by the narked expression on Rogers' face that he'd pissed him off.

Tough shit! I'm fed up with tiptoeing around when I speak to people. Look where that's got me over the years... nowhere. No, this is the new me... people need to take me as they find me or leave me the fuck alone.

"This is probably the wrong thing to say in the circumstances, but it was a pleasure meeting you. I hope things work out for you soon," Rogers said, finally extending his hand to shake.

Tim nodded and shook his hand. "Thanks for dealing with my case with sympathy and compassion."

"Our pleasure. We'll show ourselves out, let you get back to work."

"Thanks, I have dozens of calls to make."

The two men walked out of the outer office, and he pulled his shoulders back, his determination coming to the fore, and returned to his desk. There, he called his solicitor.

"Arnold, sorry to ring you off the cuff like this. I'm in need of some expert advice about the business."

"Sounds ominous. What's up, Tim?"

"The Environmental Health have been here and closed the factory down."

"They've what? Why?"

He ran through the events as they had unfolded in the last hour and then fell silent.

"Holy shit. Right, I shouldn't have to tell you of all people how serious this predicament is."

"You're right. Stop stating the obvious and tell me how the heck I'm going to get myself out of this mess."

"What does the new partner have to say about it? I'm presuming you've informed her?"

"I have. She chewed several chunks out of each of my testicles before the rats could take their share."

"Sounds like fun. Do you have any idea how this has been allowed to happen, Tim?"

"God, I wish I knew. The truth is, I don't. I even rang my former partner earlier to see if he could shed any light on what's going on. He couldn't. I'm at a loss what to do to put things right."

"Have you fallen out with anyone? Could this be a revenge attack for something you've done in the past?"

"You tell me. I really don't know. Having thought long and hard about it, I keep drawing a sodding blank. My life appears to be unravelling at breakneck speed, and I'm hopelessly lost, staring into an almighty abyss."

"Okay, calm down. We're going to need to put our heads together about this and try to find a workable solution for you to get your business up and running again, before too much damage is done."

"I'm willing to listen to any advice you have to offer, of course I am. I fear it might be too late for that, though. It's costing me thousands each minute these machines aren't churning out the products, and it seems I'm the only person who gives a hoot about that fact."

"Nonsense, not any more, Tim. I'm here and willing to give you a helping hand, but first, you need to tell me everything. I'm sensing that you're holding something back from me, am I right?"

Tim's head dipped, and he exhaled a large breath. "You've always been an astute bugger."

"I have. So, confide in me. I swear I won't judge if you've been up to no good, but I need to be aware of all the facts, no matter how grave they may be, before we can even think about putting things back together again, and I don't mean to simply plaster over the cracks, either."

Tim sat there for a while longer, scratching his head now and again. He had hoped that keeping the news of his family's plight under wraps would be his saving grace come the end. However, at the moment, he felt bereft and a lost soul, unable to think for himself. "Okay, you asked for it. What do you make of this? My family are being held hostage by a group of men. Don't ask me how many, all I know is that they appear to be eager to hurt my family, especially Amanda."

"What? Jesus, I knew there had to be something else to this. Have you informed the police?"

"Yes and no. I rang my friend, and he brought a copper here to see me. The kidnappers found out and took pleasure in punishing my family, forcing me to listen to their torment over the phone. I had to send the copper away."

"Shit! I'm sorry, Tim. What are their demands?"

"Oh, yes, that. It's simple, either I cobble together twenty million or… they'll kill my family unless I can come up with the money."

Arnold whistled. "Holy crap. And can you do it? Raise the capital against the business or your home?"

"I've managed to raise half the sum. I'm struggling to come up with the rest, unless you've got a spare ten mill lying around?"

"Sorry, no can do. I can probably get my hands on a couple of hundred at a stretch, but no more than that. What about the bank? Can't you borrow against the business?"

"Nigh impossible when you're in partnership with someone and they're supposed to be a silent partner. I can't see her agreeing to anything, not after her being so vocal about my failings as a partner about an hour ago. By what she said, I reckon she's got a spy working in the factory, reporting back to her."

"Whoa! Really? What a way to start a new budding partnership. And what was the outcome of that conversation?"

He paused to think. "I can't remember, in all honesty. That part of the day has proved insignificant compared to everything else I've encountered, including witnessing a rat running past me while I was giving the officers from EH a guided tour."

"Oh my, you have had a pig of a day, haven't you?"

"Yep, it's been one trauma after another, and I can't see a way out of it." His mobile vibrated across the desk. "Can you hold the line? I've got a call coming in on my mobile. I believe it's the kidnappers."

"Of course. Stay calm with them."

"I'm trying, but it is far from easy." He put his mobile on speaker. "Hello, this is Tim."

"Ooo… all very formal of you, Timmy boy. I see the men from EH have completed their inspection and the staff have all gone. You don't know how satisfying it is for us to see your business fold like this."

"Great, I'm glad I've managed to make someone's day for them, because my day is getting shittier by the second, thanks mainly to your input."

The kidnapper laughed. "Glad to be of service. I take it things aren't going too well for you, Timmy boy?"

"That's correct. How are my family coping? I hope you haven't hurt them since the last time I spoke to you."

"No, I've kept to my word. Your wife is here. Do you want to speak with her?"

"Of course. I need reassurance that she's doing okay."

"Tim, have you got the money yet?" Amanda asked. "Time isn't on our side now."

"It's all in hand, love. Don't worry. How are you and the kids holding up? Are they looking after you?"

Amanda refused to answer.

He regretted asking the questions, putting her on the spot like that. "Sorry, how are you all?"

"I think we're as well as can be expected, in the circumstances. Do your best to get that money, Tim."

"Don't worry, I'm doing all I can to achieve that aim, love. Hang in there."

Amanda screamed, and the phone was taken away from her.

The kidnapper came back on the line. "Remember, the clock is ticking. Try as you might, you're not going to be able to stop the hands of time, so get your finger out, Timmy boy... before it's too late."

"I'm doing my best. You try raising such a vast amount in the unrealistic timescale you've given me."

Laughter, and then the line went dead.

Tim picked up the landline phone and said, "Did you hear that?"

Arnold cleared his throat. "Fuck, man, I'd hate to be in either your shoes or Amanda's. I don't know what to suggest for the best. Is there any way you're going to be able to come up with the funds in the few hours remaining?"

"I'm running out of people I can tap up for money. The last thing I want to do is be negative, but I think I'm doomed, and that will only mean... no, I can't bear to think of what the consequences could be."

"Jesus, I wish I could help, even in a small way. My hands are tied, though."

"It's okay. I'm sorry, I didn't mean to burden you with this nightmare. All I need is for you to come up with a plan to get my business out of the mire while I concentrate on the kidnappers. I can't deal with both, not at the same time. What do you say, Arnold?"

"Hey, for you, I'll do anything. Let me delve into the legalities of what EH have done today and see where you stand with the people being in hospital, and I'll get back to you."

"Make it soon, the sands of time are running out."

"You have my word. Hang in there, Tim. I've got your back."

"I knew you wouldn't let me down. You never have done in the past."

"I intend to keep up that record. Speak to you later."

"Get back to me before the end of the day. Keep ringing me until I answer. You know what I'm up against, Arnold."

"I hear you loud and clear. Take care, pal."

Tim ended the call and took a moment to collect his thoughts before he got down to work again. Earlier, he'd made a list of possible banks to try. The names on that sheet of paper were dwindling fast, along with his hopes and dreams of getting his family back together in one piece. He pulled his sleeve back and worked out how much time he had left. Time was of the essence. Even if a bank agreed to give him the funds, he doubted if it would happen overnight. With that in mind, he concentrated on cobbling together the ten million he'd already been promised from different outlets and set about collecting the funds from each location. Hoping against hope that ten mill would be better than nothing and that the kidnappers would appreciate his predicament, accepting the money in exchange for his family.

Who am I trying to kid? But what else can I do, with time marching on and getting away from me?

CHAPTER 7

*B*y the time four-thirty came around, Tim had pulled several chunks out of his drastically thinning hair but thankfully had achieved his objective. He rang Arnold back, told him that he was heading out of the office and to contact him on his mobile with any news. Arnold had told him that he wasn't expecting there to be any news before the end of the day, which had again pissed him off. Setting that minor detail aside, he secured the factory for what he considered might be the final time and headed off to pick up the funds he'd been promised from several institutions, with the deadline at the forefront of his mind.

He was a bag of nerves, sitting alongside the holdall on his front seat which he kept adding to at every location until the ten million had all been collected. The whole thing was surreal, like something out of a crap B-movie that Netflix offered to its numerous subscribers.

The kidnapper had rung him an hour into his journey, to check on his progress and to furnish him with the location of where the drop-off, and ultimately, the exchange would take place. Tim was on his way there now, the bridge close to the Norfolk and Suffolk Aviation Museum. He didn't have a clue where that was, he was relying on his satnav not to screw up and lead him astray. The museum appeared on his right, and over to his left he could make out the bridge. He noticed a car parked in a nearby lay-by and wondered if that was the kidnappers' vehicle. It was too dark to see how many people were inside the car. His heart rate escalated the closer he got to the drop-off point. He sucked in a few calming breaths.

He pulled up in front of the bridge and waited for the occupants of the car to join him. It took a while; they were obviously keen to keep up the pressure on him. No matter how irate he felt about that, Tim did his best to let it wash over him. The only thing that mattered at this stage was handing over the money and getting his family back.

Movement alerted him. Two figures approached his car from the rear. He was in two minds whether to get out of the vehicle or stay put. In the end, he went with the latter option. A tap on the driver's window alerted him that it was now or never. Could he bluff his way out of this jam, or would he be putting his family's life in further jeopardy?

Where are they? Have they brought Amanda and the kids with them? Or are they going to take the money and deliver my family back to me later?

He lowered the window and glanced up at the two masked figures.

"Where's the money?" one of the men said.

"I need to see my family first. Where are they?"

The masked man gestured for someone in the car behind to come and join him. Tim watched the proceedings through his rear-view mirror, and his heart nearly jumped out of his chest when his wife and kids came through the darkness and into view. Eager to greet them, he attempted to get out of the car, but the kidnapper slammed his door shut again.

"Stay put until I tell you to move. The money, where is it?"

Nervously, Tim scratched his neck. "It's here. In the holdall next to me. I want my family first."

"They're coming. Don't screw with me. Hand me the twenty mill, and we'll let you drive away with your family."

Tim's hand hesitated over the handles of the holdall. All of a sudden, he felt insecure and gulped noisily.

"Is there a problem, Timmy boy?" asked the kidnapper with the sing-song voice he'd been dealing with all along.

"No... er... I mean yes, there might be."

"Hold it right there. Don't let them come any closer."

Tim checked his mirror again and was shocked to see two masked men restraining Amanda and the kids.

Shit! How do I get us out of this fix when there are four of them?

"Start talking, Tim," the kidnapper ordered.

"I... well, I did my very best, and all I could come up with was ten million. Surely that will be enough for you."

The kidnapper's fist flew at him and connected painfully with his jaw. His head lurched to the side and sprang back again.

"I fucking warned you what would happen if you didn't come up with the full amount, didn't I?"

"I'm sorry, you have to believe me, I did everything I could to obtain the funds, but not everyone was willing to oblige. The short notice was a contributing factor. They refused to let me have the money, you know, without the police being involved in the case."

"What do we do now, man? Let him have them or what?" the other masked man asked.

"Shut it. I'm trying to think. If we back down now, there's only going to be one winner—him. He has to be punished.

We can't allow him to get away with this, to treat us like imbeciles."

"But ten mill is a heck of a lot of money all the same."

"Fuck off! We agreed, all or nothing."

Tim wiggled his jaw to check it wasn't broken and replied, "But… it's all I'm going to be able to give you. My hands are tied, and now that you've seen to it that my business is no longer functioning, there's no way any of the banks will give me a loan against the business."

"I told you this would happen," the mouthy newcomer said. He prodded the other man in the chest which earned him a fist in the mouth.

"Shut the fuck up. Watch what you're saying and who you're saying it in front of, you hear me?"

"All right. You hit me again and you'll regret it. We've done our share in all of this. You can't get by without the rest of us, you'd be wise to remember that. I say we take the ten mill for now and keep the wife until he can come up with the extra funds."

"Nope, it's not going to happen," Tim said, his tone defiant.

The one in charge leaned in and said, "Like you have an option. Get out of the car."

Tim tentatively opened the door and stepped out. Cally and Lester shouted for him, and his gaze was drawn to his family. He was unsure and petrified how this was all going to end for them.

"Keep them back. Once we have the money then we'll consider what to do with the family. Tim here has seen fit to short-change us. What do you think of that, Amanda? What a husband, eh? Still think he's worth being with, do you?"

"Tim? Is this true?" Amanda screeched.

"I'm sorry. I came up with ten mill. That's a fortune in anyone else's book, apparently not these guys'."

His comment earned him a right hook to the jaw and two punches to the stomach. Amanda and the kids all cried out.

Tim picked himself up off the ground and pleaded with the guy not to hurt any of them.

"It's too late. The money, hand it over, now."

Tim reached inside the car for the holdall and gave it to the guy in charge who opened the zip to reveal the bundles of notes inside. The other man standing alongside him leaned in for a closer look and whistled.

"That'll do for me, not sure what you guys are going to do." He laughed.

"Wind your neck in. Everything is a big joke to you, isn't it? This is serious business. I need to consider what our next move is going to be."

"It's all I can get you, there's no point asking me for more," Tim whined.

His comment earnt him another couple of jabs to the stomach.

"Fuck, I've made my decision. Get them all in the car. We'll take them back to the house and decide their fate from there."

"No, I'm not going anywhere. You promised you would let my family go. Hold me hostage if you have to, but please, don't punish them further."

The kidnapper threatened to hit him again, and Tim cowered from him.

"Big man shouting the odds isn't so courageous after all. I've told you what's going to happen. Back in the car. Hand over your keys."

Tim removed the key from the ignition and placed them into the man's outstretched hand. The kidnapper lobbed the keys over his shoulder, and there was a plop in the water behind them.

"That's one less problem to deal with. In the car. Now."

He shoved Tim in the back towards his family. But they were still kept a few feet apart.

Another car appeared, and Tim and his family were separated again. Tim had his hands tied behind his back and was placed in the rear of the new car. Up front were the two kidnappers he'd been dealing with since he'd arrived.

"Please, where are you taking us? I've given you all the money I could raise. Don't hurt us."

"Wind your neck in and let me think," the main man said. He started the engine and drove off.

Tim twisted in his seat. The other car followed them. The journey took ten minutes or so to complete. At the other end, Tim was led into a detached house, standing alone out in the country. He stared at the door, waiting for Amanda and the kids to enter the house. They didn't.

Frantic, he asked, "What have you done with them? Where are they?"

"Take a seat, Timmy boy. You and I are going to have a quiet chat," the leader said, his mask and his associate's still in place.

Tim froze. The other man forced him to sit, and the main man shifted to stand a couple of inches in front of Tim, the holdall of money on the floor by his side.

"Why? Why aren't you letting my family go as agreed? You've got the money, you could get on a plane and go abroad, live it up over there with ten million in your pocket."

Tim felt the force of the man's irritation with a clout to his jaw, making it hurt even more.

"Button it. There's more where that came from, and I've already told you to keep your sodding mouth shut."

"I'm sorry, I'm anxious to know what you intend doing with me and my family."

"And you'll find out soon enough. Listen up, I ain't gonna tell you again, right?"

Tim nodded. A shuffling noise coming from the hallway made his ears prick up. Then there was quiet. "What have you done with them? I thought we would be together once you had the money."

Another double punch to the stomach and a third one to the other side of his jaw was the kidnapper's response. "Learn to follow orders, it might just save your life."

Tim nodded, fearful that his jaw wouldn't work if he tried to speak. It felt like it was broken, judging by the pain paralysing his face.

"We all know your actions this evening hold consequences. What I need to do now is work out what the punishment is going to be. I told you over the phone that if you didn't come up trumps with the goods then a member of your family was going to die."

"No, please, not one of them. If you have to take someone's life, then take mine, let them go. They don't deserve this. Neither do I, but I'm willing to accept my fate to save them."

A plastic bag was pulled over his head, and the ends tightened around his throat. With his hands tied behind his back, he could do very little to fight off the person trying to take his life. Darkness washed over him within seconds.

TIM WOKE UP. The bag had been removed, and he was lying on a thin, stained mattress by himself in what appeared to be a bedroom. He struggled to sit upright and leaned against the wall. His eyes adjusted to his surroundings. He just needed his ears to do the same. Nothing, he could hear absolutely zilch. He didn't even know if he was in the same house or not.

Shit, where are they? Where are Amanda, Cally and Lester? If the kidnappers have kil... I can't think about that, I just can't. I refuse to go there.

Tears formed and dripped onto his cheek. His jaw was stiff, although admittedly, less painful than before, so he presumed there was no lasting damage done, different to what he had thought at the time the goon had laid into him.

A noise sounded outside his room. He froze, not daring to breathe. The door opened, and in marched a masked man carrying a shop-bought sandwich and a carton of juice.

"Please, where are my family?" Tim dared to whisper.

The man placed the sandwich and drink on the floor beside him and wrenched his arms round so he could untie them. "Shut up," he sneered. "Another word and I'll make you sorry. Now eat and drink. Hurry up, I haven't got all day."

Tim ran his hand around each of his wrists, trying to rub some life back into them as they were too numb to hold anything. The man impatiently tapped his foot. Tim didn't recognise the voice, so he knew this wasn't the main man.

"I'm sorry, my wrists hurt, and I need to get some kind of feeling back into them before I can contemplate eating."

The man grunted and picked up the sandwich. He ripped it open and shoved one of the halves into Tim's gaping mouth. Tim ended up choking.

"Jesus, first you want something to eat and then you don't. I wish you'd make up your frigging mind."

Tim tried to mumble an apology, but even he was unable to decipher his words.

The man's patience had run out. He picked the rope up again and tussled with Tim's arms to secure them once more.

"Please, I'm hungry. Give me a chance to eat and drink, I'm begging you. I'll be no good to you dead, will I?"

"That's debatable. You've got five minutes, starting now. Either feed yourself or the rope goes back on and you starve. I'm not here to pander to you. Got that?"

"Yes, yes, I understand perfectly. I'm sorry to be such an inconvenience to you, that wasn't my intention at all."

The man got closer and through gritted teeth shouted, "Shut the fuck up. I'm sick to death of listening to your whining."

"I'm sorry," Tim mumbled again. He took the sandwich from the packet and nibbled on it, detesting the texture of the egg mayonnaise, his least favourite filling, and further-more, it was on white bread, which he also loathed.

The man left his side and crossed the room to the window but still kept half an eye on Tim, not that he was going anywhere with his legs bound. He gagged as he ate but knew he had to persevere, not knowing when or if he was likely to get another meal in the future. He washed it down with the orange juice, another item on his 'don't go near' food list.

"Can I bother you for some water instead?" he asked timidly.

"It ain't going to happen. Be grateful for what you've been given."

"I am. Sorry, I didn't mean it to come across that I'm not."

The man swiftly marched towards him and punched him. "I told you, I don't want to hear it. Any more and I take the food and drink with me and you won't see me again. It would be no skin off my nose, chum."

"Okay, I'll behave. I was just saying..." He stopped talking when the man raised his clenched fist.

In the end, his stomach rejected the rest of the sandwich and the drink.

"Have you finished?"

"Yes, thank you. Can I see my family now? Are they still here?"

The man remained silent while he secured Tim's hands behind his back, then he left the room and locked the door.

. . .

TIM WOKE up in the dark room, exhausted by his exertions of trying to get his arms out of their bindings to save himself. He'd apparently been asleep most of the day, and now night had fallen. As far as he knew there wasn't another soul in the house. He thought he'd heard the man's car leave soon after he'd given Tim his paltry meal, but he couldn't be sure.

Now, not for the first time, he was left wondering where his family were and if they were safe. His stomach rumbled. It had been hours since he'd been forced to consume that vile sandwich and being sick meant he was starving.

When will they return to feed me again? I hope Amanda and the kids are being treated better than me. Why is this still going on? They've got the money, what more do they bloody want?

The same questions circulated his mind for hours. There was nothing else for him to do but think. Daylight filled the bedroom. It was followed hours later by nightfall again, and still no one had appeared to give him any further food or water.

Why did I complain so much about my last meal, why?

Weakness consumed him the next day. His clothes were soiled with excrement and urine, leaving him utterly degraded and bereft. His fear notched up every time his family's fate entered his mind.

Another day came and went. Along with it, his thoughts became deranged. He put that down to lack of fluids. He'd read about people being left to survive without food and water for days and the shocking condition they'd been found in.

How long can I survive like this? Is this another form of punishment? Pushing me to my limit in order to get the other ten million out of me? They're going to have to kill me, I can't get my hands on the extra money. I've told them that over and over, and

111

they're not prepared to listen to me. Or, have they done what I suggested, taken the money and left the country? If it's the latter, where the fuck am I? Is someone likely to find me? What if they don't? What happens then? Do I simply waste away? I'm guessing not before delirium kicks in. What a frigging mess. It's the not knowing about Amanda and the kids that is going to kill me. They didn't deserve to get caught up in this... whatever this is.

He called out for help. *Why hadn't I thought of that before?* He had a feeling he was alone, out in the middle of nowhere. *I wish I'd taken more notice of where they were bringing me. Instead, I was more concerned about what was happening to my family. Now I'm all alone, at least I think I am. Have they left me here to waste away to nothing?*

Another nightfall, and then the sun came up. The weakness in his muscles had become unbearable. He no longer had a voice capable of drawing attention, even if someone did miraculously come looking for him. It was no good thinking otherwise, he was staring death in the face, and there was nothing he could do to prevent it from consuming him.

Something caught his attention downstairs, or was that his mind playing tricks on him?

"Please help me. I'm up here." His voice was barely audible even to his own ears, despite the effort he was using to get heard.

"Hello, is there anyone here?" the stranger's voice called out.

He had to do something to attract their attention, but his strength was drained and his voice was now non-existent. But he had to try, he just had to. He dropped his legs off the bed and raised them a few inches off the floor; it was all he could manage. He stamped the floor a couple of times, not knowing where the strength was coming from to carry out his actions. Then he strained an ear to listen.

Was that a creak on the stairs?

A snuffling noise sounded at the bottom of the door.

"Jasper, come away from there," a man's voice said from outside the room.

"Please, help me. Please," Tim cried out, or tried to.

The handle lowered, and the door inched open. A man wearing a checked cap poked his head into the room and gasped. He slapped a hand over his mouth and complained incoherently about the stench, then he tore across the room towards him.

Tim didn't see or hear anything else because a fresh darkness descended.

TIM WOKE up again in a sterile room, a drip inserted in his arm and a single blanket and sheet covering him. A buzzer sounded, and the door opened. A nurse entered and said thank you to a man lying in the bed opposite him.

"Cheers, Colin. It's about time he woke up." The nurse smiled down at him. "Hello, sleepyhead. How are you feeling?"

Tim tried to speak but no words came.

The nurse gave him a notebook and pen. "Write it down. Don't try to speak, not yet. You're going to need to give your body time to recover from the ordeal it has been through in the last few days."

Where am I? Tim wrote.

"In Norwich Hospital. You were found tied up in a house. I'll get the doctor to come and see you. He'll explain what's been going on while you've been unconscious."

Tim penned his response: *Thank you. Where are my family?*

The nurse gave him a smile but refused to answer what he considered to be a simple question.

"I won't be long." She poured him a glass of water from

the jug sitting on the bedside cabinet next to him. "Have a drink. Maintaining your fluid intake will speed up your recovery." With that, she left him.

The patient in the bed opposite shuffled across the ward which only contained four beds. "All right, mate? It was touch and go for you for a while. You were in a dreadful state when they brought you in. I'm Colin by the way."

Tim picked up the pen again and wrote: *Hi, I'm Tim. Has anyone been in to see me? My family, perhaps?*

"Sorry to disappoint you but no, no one has been near the place."

How many days have I been in here? was Tim's next question.

"This is your third day. You've been on the drip all this time. Still, that'll have given you all the nutrients to keep going. How are you feeling?"

Dog rough, Tim wrote. He added a smile, grateful for the man's kindness.

The door opened, and in walked a tall man, wearing a blue uniform. He had a stethoscope looped around his neck. "Ah, you're awake. Thank you, Mr Salter, you can go back to your bed now. What have I told you about walking about unaided and on your own?"

"Sorry, Doctor. It won't happen again."

The doctor nodded and drew the curtain around them once Colin had shuffled back towards his bed with the assistance of the nurse.

"Right, I'm the consultant, Dr Pullman. How are you feeling?" the doctor asked.

For the third time, Tim wrote on a new piece of paper that he was feeling terrible and weak.

Dr Pullman nodded. "Only to be expected, given your condition when you were admitted."

Tim wrote his next questions. *What's the damage? And how long am I going to be in here?*

"Ah, as long as necessary. You've had a near-death experience that is going to take you a while to recover from."

Tim scribbled down his next question. *Doctor, I don't really care about myself, I'm more concerned about my family. Do you know where they are?*

"No. I'll have to check with the nursing staff, but as far as I know, I don't think anyone has been in to see you. Is that what you meant?"

Tim shook his head and tried to speak, but the words dried up in his mouth. So, he reverted to using the pen and paper. *No, they went missing.* He stopped short of explaining the full story.

"I'm sorry to hear that. Umm... the police should be here to see you soon. I had to inform the inspector in charge as soon as you woke up."

"No, I can't involve the police," he made the mistake of whispering.

The doctor pointed at the paper. "I didn't catch that. Jot it down for me."

Tim started to write but then stopped. What was the point? His family were still missing, and he needed the police to help find them, didn't he?

"Are you okay?" the doctor checked.

Tim closed his eyes and rested his head against the pillow, exhaustion catching up with him after his exertions.

"You rest. I'll wake you when the police get here."

Tim kept his eyes closed until he heard the curtain rings slide back and forth on the pole. *I have to get out of here before the cops show up, otherwise every hope I have of getting my family back will go out of the window.*

He must have drifted off to sleep because a little while later the curtains swooshing back woke him. Tim rubbed his eyes, wondering if he might still be asleep and dreaming when he saw the person who was standing in front of him.

"Tim, it's good to see you again," DI Bob Addis said. He sat in the chair next to the bed.

There was a young female at his side who he assumed to be a junior-ranking officer.

Tim shook his head and closed his eyes.

"Come now, Tim, before I was prepared to take a step back and allow you to do things your way and look how that turned out."

Tim picked up his pen and paper. *I don't care. I have to do things my way, or they'll kill them.*

"Have you seen your family since they were taken?"

Yes, briefly. Then they were whisked away from me, Tim wrote.

"Do you know why? Why you were left to die in that deserted house?"

I don't. But I need to find them, and if the kidnappers get wind of the police being involved, it's only going to signify their death, isn't it? he wrote, his wrist now aching.

"Not necessarily. Give me a chance."

Tim paused and tried to get his thoughts into some semblance of order, then he scribbled down another sentence. *But the kidnappers knew you were there, at the factory.*

Addis shot a glance at the officer beside him and faced Tim again. "But how?"

I don't know. They knew about everything that day. The Environmental Health showed up as well, not only with complaints about people in hospital dealing with food poisoning but they also found rats on the premises, too. It was all a deliberate act, sabotage if you will, to get my factory closed down.

"I'm sorry to hear that. How did they kidnap you?"

They set up a meeting point to carry out the exchange, the money for my family, except...

Addis read what Tim had written on the notebook and stared at him. "But… things didn't go according to plan, did they?"

No, the money was ten million short. That's when they separated me from my family, and I haven't seen or heard from them since. Tears misted his vision, preventing him from writing anything else. He wiped his eyes with his hands and wrote, *They could be dead for all I know.*

"Let's not think negatively about the issue, not yet. Are you willing to get us involved now? In my opinion, I think your options are limited or virtually zero at this stage. They left you for dead. They're not the type you can deal with on your own, they're too dangerous. Surely that's hit home by now, hasn't it?"

Tim sighed and nodded. *I suppose you're right. I don't know where to begin looking. The house where I was found, where was it?*

"It was an abandoned farm out near Flixton. Do you know that area?"

No, I was told to meet them at the Aviation Museum out that way, near the bridge. Then they took me to the house, fed me for one day and then left me alone. I can't tell you how many days I was there, everything is such a muddle. I think delirium through lack of food and water set in. He shook out his wrist again after he finished writing and showed Addis his reply on the notebook.

"I'm sorry they've put you through this. I can't force you to accept our help, only you can make that decision."

Tim stared ahead of him. Weighing up his options drained him, and he rested his head back on the pillow.

"Tim?" Addis prompted.

He raised his head and nodded. "What have I got to lose?" he mouthed.

Bob Addis gave him the thumbs-up. "That's the spirit. Do you know what day you met them at the museum?"

He mulled it over and then wrote, *I think it was Wednesday. It was the same day EH showed up at the factory. You can check with them, can't you?*

"Yes, we'll do that. Is there anything else significant you can remember that you think might either give us an indication of who we're dealing with or where they might have taken your family?"

Frustrated, Tim wrote, *Do you think I'd still be in here if I could?*

"Fair enough. Right, can you jot down your address for me? Once the doctor is satisfied that you're fit to go home, I'll ensure there is a copper on duty at the property, with you at all times."

You reckon they'll contact me again? Won't they think I'm already dead?

"If, like you say, they've known your moves all along, I'm surmising they'll know you've been rescued by now."

Shit, I hadn't thought about that, and here I am, talking to you. That's only going to prove harmful to my family.

"We won't know the answer to that until the kidnappers get in touch. Did you pick up anything from the conversations you overheard between them, about what they intended to do with the money?"

No, I suggested they take the ten mill and leave the country. Whether they did that or not is anyone's guess. I just want my family back, and quickly, if they're still alive.

"We want the same thing, I assure you. I'm going to let you get some rest now. Will you give us the permission we need to search your house? Do you have a key?"

No, it was with my car keys, and the bastards threw them in the river near the museum. Can you check if my car is still out there? It's a Merc 300 SL.

"We'll get on it right away. Does a neighbour have a key to the property? Or should we break down the door?"

Number ten, Donna, she has a spare key, she's a friend of Amanda's. God, she's going to be devastated by the news, she adores our kids.

"We'll do our best to break the news to her gently. Right, is there anything else?"

No. I think that's everything. Hopefully, I'll get my voice back soon.

"Good luck with that. Rest now. I'll keep you up to date with the investigation. Here's my card. Ring me if you need to… umm… speak to me."

They both stared at each other and smiled.

I get what you mean. Can you work your magic on the doctor, sort out an early release date for me?

"Don't be in a hurry to discharge yourself. Your body needs time to recover from the ordeal it has been through."

I know, but I don't care about myself. My family and getting them back home with me is my priority. It has to be, they're all I've got now that my business has folded.

Addis raised a finger and slowly wagged it. "Don't lose hope on that front, either. Now you've allowed us to become involved, I'm sure EH will take a different stance on what's been going on at the factory. From what I can tell, none of this is your fault."

Isn't it? I find that hard to believe, Tim wrote.

"I'll be in touch soon."

Tim watched them leave, and his heart sank.

Have I done the right thing, getting them involved? What can I do to find my family, lying here in a hospital bed? My life is a bloody mess. I have to admit defeat sooner or later and realise I can't do this alone. Maybe if I had crumbled and got them on board in the first place… maybe all this could have been avoided. Who the hell knows?

He rested his head back, closed his eyes and fell asleep.

119

CHAPTER 8

*T*im was released from hospital a few days later and, true to his word, Addis placed a member of his team at the house with him for the first couple of days, which ended up being a welcome relief. Tim broke out in hives at the thought of being alone, rambling around the huge house with his family still on the missing list. It was filled with happy memories, so what did he expect?

Addis also kept to his word about frequently updating him as the investigation proceeded. He'd put out a statement through the press about the kidnapping but regrettably had received very little response from the general public. However, what Tim was also relieved about was that the kidnappers hadn't been in touch to make further financial demands. But there was a flip side to that concept, too; it meant the kidnappers hadn't reached out to confirm they were still holding his family, either. So in that respect, they were no further forward.

Two days after leaving the hospital, Tim signed for a registered letter. He tore it open, thinking it was from the kidnappers. It wasn't. It was from the bank, threatening to repossess the house if he didn't make the first payment on the loan he had taken out. He felt mortified and hung out to dry. *How can I fight them? I have no business I can offer as collateral any more. Everything I own is here, and now they're threatening to take that away from me.*

DI Addis had shown up at the house not long after and caught him mid-meltdown. "If there's anything else I can do, just ask," he said, once Tim had shared the unfavourable news.

"You can tell me what you're doing to find my family," Tim said, now his voice had fully recovered.

"Everything we can. I must admit, I was very disappointed by the lack of response we received from the public. No one saw anything the day you met your family. I do have some good news for you, though."

Tim inclined his head, his hopes rising a touch. "What's that?"

Addis held out his palm to reveal the keys of Tim's home and car. "These are yours, I believe."

"And that's it? How do you expect me to react? Jump for joy? Do a happy dance for you?"

Addis's expression had clouded over before his eyes, and he regretted his snarky comment.

"I'm sorry, you'll have to forgive my lack of enthusiasm. To me the car is just a possession that will be taken into consideration when the bank come knocking on my door for their money."

"Let me have a word with them, see if I can stall things for you. Have EH been in touch?"

"Yes, they're having a meeting, debating whether they're going to allow the factory to open or not. I'm in two minds to tell them to shove it. It's not like I've got any staff still on the books to run the place. They'll have probably found other employment by now, won't they?"

"Have you asked them?"

Tim held his arms out to the sides. "You think I've had the time?"

"No, I guess not. Don't lose hope, Tim. We're working hard to find your family. The clues are proving difficult to find at the moment, but that won't prevent us from trying."

"That's good to hear. Well, if there's nothing else, I'm going to need to start ringing round what mates I've got left, see if any of them can put me up for a while. I'm going to need to start selling off the furniture et cetera around here, as well. It's not like I've got the funds to pay a removal firm and have the stuff shifted and put into storage, is it?"

"I'm sorry your back is against the wall, Tim."

"Yes, so you keep saying. I can deal with this crap. All you've got to do is track down my family and then we'll be laughing, won't we? Well, sort of. I'll be homeless and unemployed but at least I'll have my loved ones around me once more."

"Let's make that happen. I'll touch base with you soon."

Tim saw him to the door and watched him drive away. Then he returned to the living room and sat on the couch. The officer on duty at the house brought him a cup of coffee.

"Here you go, Tim. Try not to get too despondent," Warren said.

"I'm trying, believe me. It's getting harder each day, though. What would you do in my shoes?"

Warren sat on the arm of the easy chair and sipped at his drink. "That's a difficult one. I don't envy you, not in the slightest. It's not like you can throw yourself into work to distract yourself, can you?"

"Exactly. All I've got to occupy my day is to sit here, constantly fretting over my family's dilemma. It's driving me insane. I should be out there, tearing Norfolk apart to try and find them."

Warren shook his head. "It wouldn't do any good. I promise you, our guys will be doing their bit, scouring the streets in between dealing with the other criminals circulating the area."

"Are you sure about that? I've got my doubts."

"About how the investigation is going as a whole? Or is there something else you're unhappy about?"

"Let's just say Addis isn't filling me with confidence at this time."

"He's between a rock and a hard place, you must realise that. It would appear the kidnappers have gone to ground. He'll be calling on all his contacts for help, I can assure you."

"If you say so. In the meantime, my whole world is crumbling around me, and there's not a damn thing I can do to stop it. I'm well and truly fucked, and for what? This is still mind-boggling to me, how all this came about. My family being kidnapped, just to extort money from me, and by who? That's the frigging frustrating part, I have no fucking idea who the heck is behind this. I swear, if I knew that, he or they, wouldn't still be walking the streets, and I'd be serving time for their murders."

"I'm right there beside you, Tim. I'm sure I'd feel exactly the way you do if I were in your shoes. Take my word for it, Addis feels the same, as well. Give him and his team a chance. There's a lot to sift through, and with very few clues or evidence to hand, it makes it a very complex case to deal with. He won't let you down, none of us will."

Tim nodded and sipped his drink. "I need to go for a walk. Do you want to stay here or tag along for some fresh air?"

"Why not? It's a fresh but sunny day out there, a stroll will help blow the cobwebs away, won't it?"

They left the house a few minutes later. Tim was right, the walk did him the world of good. He could see why people were encouraged to get out into the big wide world, to keep their mental health on the straight and narrow. "Do you get much exercise? Mental stimulation? You must have a job that has you pulling your hair out at times."

"I try to get out and about when I can. I think it's necessary and we have stunning countryside all around us, we'd be foolish not to take advantage of it, right?" Warren replied.

"Absolutely. I try to get the kids out into the fresh air when I can. It's not always easy, not when all they want to do is sit in their bedrooms playing on the Xbox or their damn computers all day long."

"Totally different to our day, right? God, I sound like my father now."

They both laughed. "You're not wrong, I was always out kicking a ball around when I was growing up, you barely see that these days. What does your wife do?"

"She's an admin clerk at the station. Most weeks her schedule is easier than mine. So, most of the childcare falls on her shoulders."

"Kids… as parents we're always complaining about them, but it's times such as this that we're able to take a step back and appreciate what they really mean to us. I feel disoriented without them."

Warren slapped him on the back. "I can't even begin to imagine the torment you must be going through, Tim. If ever you need to vent, feel free. I think opening up to someone will be good for you."

"Thanks. Is that a new job role for you? Being a shrink on the side?"

They both laughed again and continued their wander alongside the winding river.

"It's the little things in life that I miss," Tim said. "The sound of my kids laughing, the loud whispering of them in their bedrooms, asking each other if they're asleep. On the other hand, what I don't miss is all the petty squabbling they used to get up to. I'm sure deep down they truly love each other, but when they're in full flow, I used to dread coming home some days in case they had throttled each other."

"Mine are the same. I have a boy and a girl, as well. Maybe it would be different if they were the same gender. I guess we'll never find that out. Perhaps, in the circumstances, your kids' relationship will improve."

"I'd like to hope so. They appeared to be scared out of their minds, the brief glimpse I caught of them." Tim fell silent, that image haunting him for several moments. He stopped walking and stared at the water gently rippling as it hit part of the riverbank jutting out.

"Are you okay, Tim?" Warren asked after a while.

"I don't know, am I? I don't think I'll ever be okay again, not while they're still out there, in the hands of the kidnappers, if they still have them. For all I know, when the bastards left me to rot in that house, they probably killed the kids and Amanda and dumped their bodies where no one is likely to find them. Doubtless down an old mineshaft or disused well. Are there any mineshafts around here?" he asked, unsure if he was making any sense or not.

Warren shrugged. "You tell me, I'm not sure in this area."

Tim picked up a stick from the bank at his feet and threw it into the river. It floated downstream, taking a piece of his heart with it. Many a time, he'd brought the kids down here when they were younger—actually, when the house was being constructed. They'd played pooh sticks at different parts of the river, sometimes up by the bridge and others where the two rivers merged into one, half a mile downstream. Tears emerged, and he soon lost his focus on the stick.

"Come on, maybe we should get back to the house. The clouds are getting blacker, we don't want to get caught out.

125

Neither of us thought about grabbing a coat," Warren reminded him.

"You're right. I've had enough of living in the past, it's not getting me anywhere. I must remain in the present and look to the future, whatever that might be."

As they began their short amble up the drive to Tim's mansion, Warren grasped his arm.

"Wait here."

"What? Why?" Tim stared at the open front door and soon realised what the young officer was talking about. "Shit. I shut that on the way out, I'm sure I did."

"You did. I saw you do it. Don't worry. I'll get on the phone, call for backup. Stay here, Tim. In fact, go and stand by the garage, out of the way, just in case there's someone in there and they make a run for it."

"If they do, I'll pounce on the fuckers."

Warren withdrew his Taser and pointed to where he expected Tim to take cover. Reluctantly, Tim agreed and dashed across the gravel, his gaze never leaving the front door. Once he was tucked up beside the garage, he surveyed the area. The builders had left some unwanted equipment there that he's been trying to get them to shift for months. At the bottom of the pile was a rusting metal pole. He dislodged it from its hidey-hole and tested it in his hands.

This will do. I'll get the buggers if they get past Warren.

A siren sounded in the distance, and a patrol car showed up within a few minutes of Warren placing the call.

"Hey, Steve, glad you were around the corner. We came back from a stroll by the river to find the door open. I'm here keeping an eye on the bloke; his wife and kids have been kidnapped."

"Right, I can see your apprehension about going in there alone. Have you had a chance to check around the back?"

"No, thought I'd stay here until you guys arrived, just in case the fuckers bolted past me."

"Let's get in there and see what's going on, then."

Tim watched the three officers, all armed with Tasers, enter the house.

Sod this, I'm not staying here.

With a tight grip on the pole, he followed the three officers up the steps and into the entrance hall. He stayed there, listening to the men warn any likely intruders that they were the police and to show themselves.

A few seconds later, the three men came back into the hallway.

"I told you to stay put," Warren said.

"I'll check upstairs," one of the uniformed officers said. He tutted as he darted past Tim and ran up the stairs two at a time.

"I'm sorry, I presumed there wasn't anyone in the house," Tim mumbled.

Steve appeared behind them. "Nothing in either of the other rooms downstairs, and the back door was still locked."

"Right, cheers."

"All clear up here," the other officer said.

Warren nodded and turned his attention to Tim. "Let's go back in the lounge. You're going to need to have a look around, see if anything has been taken, or maybe left for that matter."

"I'll try. I'm not the most observant person to ever walk this earth."

Tim led the way back into the lounge and began scanning all the surfaces for any kind of clue. He found nothing in that room or the dining room. However, it was a different story in the kitchen. Sitting on the worktop, close to the kettle, he found a note. He went to reach for it, but Warren slapped his hand away.

"Don't touch it, not until you've got gloves on. There might be prints on there we can use."

"Sorry, I wasn't thinking."

Steve removed a pair of nitrile gloves from his pocket and handed them to Tim. He struggled to get his fingers into one of them. Frustrated, Warren snatched the gloves off him and slipped his hands in instead.

"Let's see what we've got here." Warren opened the folded note that had been placed in a tent shape by the kettle and read it aloud. "*So, Timmy boy, you survived. The question is, DID YOUR FAMILY?*"

Tim cringed as soon as Warren read the words *Timmy boy*. There was no doubt in his mind who the note was from. "Shit. Let the games begin, eh? How much fucking more do I have to put up with before they hand my family back to me?"

"All right. I'm going to need you to stay strong, Tim. We'll get this note over to the lab ASAP, see if they can find anything on it."

Tim felt numb, and his legs wobbled. Warren took a photo of the note on his phone and asked Steve to put it in an evidence bag.

"Can you guys drop it off at the lab on your way back to the station?"

"Sure," Steve replied. He extracted a bag from one of his pockets, shook it out and popped the note inside. "Leave it with us. Do you need us to hang around, or shall we make a move now?"

"If everywhere is clear then, yes, you make tracks. I'll lock the door after you. Are you all right, Tim? Can you make it into the lounge?"

"Yes, I think so, if my legs will carry me."

"Steve, give us a hand." Warren gestured for the officer to stand on the other side of Tim and, together, they helped him to the leather sofa in the lounge.

"I'll be fine. Thanks." Embarrassment swathed him. *What the fuck is wrong with me?*

As if answering Tim's unspoken question, Warren sat beside him and patted him on the knee. "It's to be expected. This will have come as a huge shock to you. You're not fully recovered yet, having just been discharged from hospital."

"Yes, it's definitely taken the wind out of my sails. My torment is never-ending. Why are they doing this to me? I've got nothing left for them to take. The house will be gone soon. I'm going to be declared homeless and bankrupt by the end of the month, for fuck's sake. Now I don't know if my family are still alive or not. I can't stand them playing with me. I'd rather know the truth."

"Bastards. I feel for you, Tim. I'm going to give DI Addis a call, make him aware of what's happened. All I ask is that you hang in there, mate. Don't let the fuckers win."

Tim raised an eyebrow. "They did that a long time ago. They've set out to ruin my life, that much is evident. Well, they get full marks from me for achieving their aim."

Warren smiled, patted him on the knee again and walked to the other side of the room to make the call. He turned his back on Tim, making it impossible to either hear what he was whispering or to read his lips.

Helplessness descended, and he couldn't see any way out of the situation. *Have they still got my family or not? Why? Why haven't they released them yet? Why are they hanging around? To try and get the extra ten mill out of me? And if that money isn't forthcoming, what happens then?*

"Tim, I said, are you okay?"

"Sorry, I was distracted. I've got dozens of questions I need to know the answers to pinging around my head."

Warren sat close to him again. "Try and remain calm. Don't let them wind you up. Addis is on his way back to see you."

"Why? What can he do? Except offer me empty promises. I need you guys to get out there and find these bastards. To rescue my family, bring them back to me. Why is it proving so difficult?"

"You're going to have to bear with us, Tim. These guys are obviously pros. If they don't want to be found, then there's little we can do about it. I swear, Addis and the team will be doing their utmost to track them down. Let's see what the lab comes up with regarding the note."

"They'll probably have worn gloves, especially if, as you say, they're professionals."

"It only takes one minor slip-up to sink them. Leave the worrying to us. You just concentrate on getting yourself better."

"Why? To build my strength up for the next battle, you mean?"

"Not necessarily. Neither of us knows what lies ahead, Tim. I'm going to need you to dig deep and trust the process. Hang on to the fact that your family will be at the end of it."

"Yeah, but will they be dead or alive?"

Warren shrugged. "I have an inkling all will be revealed shortly. There's a reason they've got in touch, to let you know they're still around. I'm sure it will come out soon."

Tim sat back, shaking his head over and over, his thoughts turning dark and sinister, but he was determined not to air his concerns in case they came true.

ADDIS RETURNED to the house half an hour later, and Warren showed him the photo of the note.

"How did they get into the house?" Addis demanded.

Tim could tell the inspector was put out, having to come back so soon. "We locked the front door when we went out for a walk down by the river. It was open when we came back."

"Haven't you thought about changing the locks?" Addis asked.

Tim shot a glance at Warren and then replied to Addis. "With respect, I've not long come out of hospital, it's not something that was high on my to-do list."

"Well, it should have been. Maybe I'm at fault for not advising you to do it as a matter of priority. Warren, you should have jogged my memory or actioned it yourself."

"Yes, sir, I agree. It's very remiss of me. I'll be more aware next time."

"Next time? Get it done ASAP. We'll pay for it if that's a concern for Mr Farrant."

"Thank you," Tim muttered. His chin dipped and rested on his chest.

Warren left the room.

Tim sighed. "Don't take it out on him, this is my fault, not his."

"It's no one's *fault*. I'm not in the habit of blaming members of my team, it's something we should have all considered the minute you came out of hospital, or possibly while you were still in there. I'm guilty of taking my eye off the ball."

"You've been dealing with other things. What do you think they want from me now? I've told them there are no further funds. This place will be gone by the end of the month."

"They don't know that, though, do they? They probably think you can sell this for a fair whack to top up the money you've already handed to them."

"Christ, they've got another think coming. I'm screwed. Will this put my family in further danger? I haven't spoken to them; I don't even know if they're still alive."

"That's what you need to do. If they ring you, or make further contact with you, get proof of life. You're going to have to be tough, remain determined with them if they get in touch, demand to speak with either Amanda or the children."

"Blimey, I'll do my best. It's not going to be easy, not with the kind of crap that's going round in my head. What if they don't make contact with me? What then?"

"They will. That's what all this has been about today. They're keen to keep you dangling. Ready to yank your chain at a moment's notice. Don't worry, we'll be by your side every step of the way."

"And how long is that going to last? Indefinitely?"

Addis shook his head. "No, we haven't got the funds to stick around for long. I want to assure you, my team are working day and night to find these bastards. My contacts are doing their bit, too. Don't give up on us, not yet, Tim."

"I have no intention of giving up on you. Let's face it, you're all I've got."

"When you're feeling up to it, we're going to need to put our heads together and try to source the cause of the issue."

Tim frowned. "Meaning what?"

"There must be a reason the kidnappers chose you and your family. We're going to need to figure out what that reason is."

"Damn, I've thought about nothing else since this whole episode began, well, maybe getting all the funds together took up a smidgen of my time, in the beginning. But day and night, I keep going over what has gone on in the past six months and all I'm doing is drawing a blank."

"What about your old partner?"

"Matt?" Tim chewed on his lip. "I've debated that long and hard and decided he wouldn't have the balls to do anything like this. He'd have no reason to. I spoke to him the other day; he's living it up in the Caribbean on the proceeds he got from selling off his share of the business."

Addis stared at him and hitched up a shoulder. "It's not unknown for people to get greedy. I'll do some digging into his past if you give me his name and address."

Tim shot out of his seat and removed a notebook and pen from the sideboard, then returned to the sofa. He jotted down Matt's details, still shaking his head in disbelief. "I'd be surprised if you found anything on him."

"Something is better than nothing, as they say. In my vast experience, the slightest niggle can lead to an almighty revelation, one that can knock people sideways. Let's put it this way, we've got very little else to go on at present. I'm going to need a list of any competitors you've had problems with over the past couple of years, too. Didn't you recently launch a new range?"

A whirlwind started spinning in Tim's mind. "Jesus, no way. They wouldn't dare, would they?"

Addis inclined his head. "I'm guessing that everyone struggled during the financial crash, businesses large and small alike. Are you telling me that didn't happen in the chocolate-making industry?"

"Initially, sales dipped slightly, but they recovered quickly. We ended up being busier than we were before the financial dip."

"What about your competitors?"

"I can't speak for them. I suppose it depends on how they coped during the manufacturing process, if they had enough staff to cope with the extra shifts we were all expected to put in." This got Tim thinking, something he'd neglected to do previously. "Shit, yes, now I've had time to think about things, Foulds and Sons nearly went under not long after the crash."

"I'm going to need their details."

"Adrian Foulds took over from his father. He's the type to blame his failings on others instead of owning up to his mistakes." Tim jotted down the address of the factory that, from what Matt had told him in the past month or so, was only just surviving.

"Interesting. There are plenty of people like him walking the streets, I can tell you. I'm not saying it will come to anything, but it's a start. I haven't wanted to push you for information up until now, but taking everything into consideration and what has occurred today, I think it's imperative to know all the facts. I don't profess to know the ins and outs of what goes on in a factory, so anything you want to share with me at this time could prove beneficial to the investigation."

"I'm trying to think. I had a happy ship at the factory, I can't see anything being wrong there, although..."

"Although? I'm going to need to hear it all, Tim, you know, while you're on a roll."

Warren returned to the fold. He and Addis took a seat while Tim racked his brains.

"I'm going back to before I was taken, you know, around the time the Environmental Health bods showed up at my door. When I met my new partner, she hinted that she had spies within the factory. Come to think of it, so did the kidnappers. So, perhaps there might be something in that."

"Have you employed any new staff lately?" Addis asked.

Warren had his pen poised over his notebook.

"Not that I can think of."

"Okay, well, if that's the case then we're looking at someone being offered a vast sum of money to do the spying for either the kidnappers or the new partner. Can you think of anyone who had money troubles and might be forced to go down that route?"

Tim mulled over the question for a few moments. "I can't think of anyone, no. But then..."

"But then? Go on, don't stop there, Tim."

"I was going to say the factory workforce aren't the best-paid people in the country, but I do what I can for the staff, add incentive bonuses here and there. No, I can't believe it would be one of them. They've been with me a while and they all seemed happy enough. No gripes in recent months from what I can recall."

"I think we should still interview them all. It's surprising what gets revealed when people are put under pressure by the police."

"Goodness, really? Crap, I haven't got all their details with me. I'll have to nip into the factory later."

"In your own time, however, today would be preferable. Warren will tag along, help you to gather all the information. Try and get it back to me by the end of the day, if you would."

Tim rose from his seat. "We can go now. I don't feel like being stuck in the house, knowing those bastards have been here today."

Warren held his hand up. "Whoa, we're going to have to go later, I've arranged for a locksmith to come over soon."

Tim flopped into his seat again. "Oh, I wasn't aware of that. I can try and draw up a list of names here and fill in the details when we get there. Depends on how rusty my memory is."

"No pressure," Addis said. "Why don't you leave it until you get back to the factory? Okay, if there's nothing else, I'm going to head back to the station, get my team doing the necessary background checks on Foulds before I head over there and have a word with him myself."

. . .

135

WITH THE LOCKS changed a few hours later, Tim and Warren secured the house and drove to the factory. As it loomed into sight ahead of them, a shiver of trepidation trickled down Tim's spine.

"I can't say I'm looking forward to venturing inside."

"May I ask why? The kidnappers haven't been here, have they?"

"No. But they've contacted me here, put me on edge. Plus, I had to do the dirty deed and lay off all the staff. Then there was the issue of the rats and the EH to deal with. It was a bloody nightmare, not something I had the intention of revisiting anytime soon, and yet… here we are."

"Out of necessity, Tim, you need to remember that. Without the information we've come here for, the investigation will dry up quicker than a nun's… no, sorry, I shouldn't have started that sentence."

They both laughed.

"Thanks for trying to cheer me up. How do you do this day in, day out?"

"Do what?" Warren asked.

He drew up into the parking place nearest to the factory door, and they exited the car.

"Babysit people when they're at their lowest ebb?"

"It comes naturally. I'm one of life's good guys. Willing to lend an ear or a helping hand if it'll ease any issue a person in need might have."

"You're a pleasure to know, Warren. It's not often I've said that over the years."

"Gee, thanks. I'm only doing my job, Tim. Come on, less praise on your part and more action." Warren held out his hand for the keys.

He unlocked the door, and Tim punched in his number to turn off the alarm.

"I bet that'll scare the crap out of any rats if they're still on site."

Tim shuddered. "Did you have to mention those blighters? They give me the bloody willies. If they're still around, and there's no reason why they shouldn't be, I bet they've multiplied by the dozen by now. Christ, why did I have to say that? Horrible bloody creatures. Any idea how I can get rid of them?"

"A call to the council might be in order."

"I'll add it to my extensive to-do list which is getting longer by the minute. We'll head straight upstairs; I think we'll be safer up there. I don't think they can climb stairs, or can they?"

"You tell me. I'm not an expert in vermin activity, not the four-legged kind."

They made it to the stairs without encountering any unwanted inhabitants. Tim kept his focus ahead of him; it would have been too upsetting for him to have seen the machinery to his right that had disastrously been forced to come to a standstill.

"It must be heartbreaking for you to see everything come to a grinding halt?" Warren said. He paused halfway up.

Tim continued on his journey, refusing to stop. "Yeah, let's not go there." He walked along the corridor and entered his secretary's office, then on to his own. Opening the door, he was taken aback by the mess. Papers and furniture strewn everywhere. "Jesus, what the fuck? This is going to be a nightmare to sort through."

Warren came up behind him, said a few curse words under his breath and squeezed Tim's shoulder. "We've got this. Don't let the fuckers get to you."

"I need to get the coffee machine fired up; we're going to need it. Where the fuck do we begin?"

"I'll get the coffee organised, and you make a start on this crap."

Tim stood there, taking in all the paperwork that had been emptied out of the filing cabinet. "What the bloody hell could they have been after? Why come in here and wreck the place? How the hell did they get in?"

"How many people have a key to the factory?" Warren asked. He seemed frustrated by the coffee machine.

Tim crossed the room and took over the task. "Two people have keys. The new owner and my factory manager."

"Can you give them a call, see if they've both got their keys?"

After he filled the machine with water and filter coffee, Tim removed his phone from his pocket and rang his manager. "Gary, hi, it's Tim. Have you got a second for a chat?"

"All the time in the world now I've been given my cards. How are things with you, boss? The last I heard you were in hospital."

"I'm getting there. Sorry about the job. If I ever get things up and running again, you'll be the first one I contact, I promise."

"It's foolish to make promises you're not going to be able to fulfil."

"My old mum had a motto, never say never. Anyway, I don't suppose you've still got your keys to this place, have you?"

"Somewhere. I was supposed to have dropped them off last week, but what with you being in hospital I wasn't sure what to do. They're here, I've just got to lay my hands on them."

"Can you ring me back if you find them?"

"Of course."

"Speak later."

Tim hit the disconnect button and dialled Barbara's number.

"And what do you want?" she said.

"Hi, Barbara, I thought I'd give you a call to give you an update on the situation."

"Well, get on with it."

"The EH shut the business down as you know. My family are still missing. The kidnappers held me hostage for three to four days. I'm lucky to be alive."

"And?" she said snootily.

"And, my business has gone and…"

"You mean *our business*, surely. About that. It's in the hands of my solicitors, I'm suing you. You should be hearing from them soon."

"What? I haven't got any money to pay you, so what would be the point in suing me? Have a bloody heart, woman."

"This is business. I'm utterly professional, there's no place for sentiment. I became your partner for a reason, to make money, not lose it. There, you have it on a plate, do with it what you want."

"Fine, you've made your position perfectly clear. I forgot to add that the police are involved in the case now, after my near-death experience that you've just showed lack of compassion for. They'll be in touch soon."

She gasped.

He ploughed on, ignoring her, "They've also instructed me to give you a call, to ask if you still have the keys of the factory. As you recall, I sent them to you after Matt gave me his set back."

"You did?"

"Yes, I had the parcel tracked, and they were signed for at your address. Can you check they're still with you?"

"I'll do my best. Is there a specific reason why you're asking?"

"Because someone has been here, in the factory without my authorisation, and there are only two other people who hold the keys. Another fact that I have passed on to the police."

"I haven't been near the place, if that's what you're insinuating."

"Well, someone has."

"You'd be foolish to blame me, I'm warning you."

"Ah, I'd be foolish, would I? I have news for you. All this started when you joined the company, another important detail the police appear to be very interested in."

"What? Are you pointing the finger at me for all of the problems you appear to have brought upon yourself?"

"I'm not. But over the years I've learnt that the facts, good or bad, don't lie."

Barbara growled something indecipherable down the line and then slammed the phone down.

Tim punched the air, considered he'd got one over on the woman, but one glance at Warren's face told a very different story.

Warren shook his head and tutted. "We never apprise the enemy that we're on their tail, if indeed she is part of this. All you've succeeded in doing is forewarning her. She'll be over there now, covering her tracks. Let's face it, you'd do the same in her position, wouldn't you? I know I would."

Tim sank to his knees in the middle of the paperwork surrounding him. He was drowning fast, whichever way he cared to look at it.

CHAPTER 9

 resent Day

SALLY'S MIND was all over the place. She had spent the last few days going over the details of the Farrant case, and the team were none the wiser, until Stuart discovered a newspaper article that was supposed to be a follow-up to the original story the paper had run. In it, it stated that Tim was still searching for his family.

"What the fuck? When was this printed, Stuart?"

"Two months after the original story was put out there, boss."

"That poor man. If you compare the old and new pictures of him, there's a horrifying stark contrast," Sally replied.

Lorne joined in the conversation. "There's bound to be, if he had been living on his nerves for a few months. Does it have his new address there?"

"No, not from what I can tell by scan reading the article. I'll go over it once more," Stuart said.

Sally sighed and leaned against the wall beside her. "We need to find him and we're running out of options."

"I think I might have stumbled across something, boss," Joanna called across the room.

Sally darted over to Joanna's desk. "You have? What's that?"

"I've got a vehicle registered to a Timothy Farrant, which might be him."

"It's got to be worth a punt. Jot down the address, and Lorne and I will pay him a visit." Her stomach clenched into a tight knot. "I have a good feeling about this, folks. Keep up the excellent work. You've made great progress so far, given the minimal amount of evidence we've had to go on."

Joanna smiled and wrote down the address then handed it to Sally. "All in a day or two's work."

"Thanks, Joanna. You guys never cease to amaze me with the tenacity you show once you have the bit between your teeth."

"IS THIS THE ADDRESS?" Sally peered over the steering wheel and took in her surroundings, in particular the run-down property which was slap bang in the middle of a terrace of similar-looking properties, set in the worst part of town.

"If it is, my heart goes out to the bloke. His old house was luxurious. What a bloody come-down for the poor bugger."

"Exactly." Sally shuddered without intending to and exited the car. She met up with Lorne on the pavement and ensured she locked the car properly at least three times.

"You make me laugh. Once would have been enough. What are you expecting to find when we come out? The car up on jacks and the tyres missing?"

"You can't be too careful in these types of neighbourhoods. One whiff that we're coppers, and the arseholes won't think twice about wrecking the car, take my word for it."

Lorne tutted and sniggered. "You would never have coped being a copper on the streets of London."

"I fear you're right. I have no regrets; this car means a lot to me."

"It's a possession. Think of the poor man we're about to visit, he's lost everything, as far as we know."

"Don't. I can't say I'm looking forward to telling him we believe we've discovered his wife's remains. Umm... feel free to jump in and deliver the devastating news for me."

"I'll pass, thanks all the same."

"Charming, there was me thinking you'd have my back, you know, slip into Jack's role with ease."

Lorne laughed. "Don't pull that one on me."

"It doesn't matter. I spy, I think we've been spotted. Are you up for this?"

"As I'll ever be. Good luck."

Sally took the lead up the short path to the front door. She covered her finger with the sleeve of her jacket to ring the bell. The man who had been at the window seconds earlier opened the door.

"Hello, can I help?"

Sally was aghast by his appearance. The photos she'd seen of him bore no resemblance to the man standing before them. She fished out her warrant card and introduced herself and Lorne. "DI Sally Parker, and this is my partner, DS Lorne Warner, Mr Farrant. May we come in and speak with you?"

"Not until you tell me what this is about." He pulled the door against his shoulder, closing the gap behind him.

"It's a delicate matter. Please, we wouldn't be asking if we didn't feel it was important. It would be better if we spoke to you in private."

He groaned and let out an impatient breath. "If you must.

You're going to have to take me as you find me. Life hasn't been easy the past few years. Not that I'm making excuses. We need to get on with it, put up with the hand we've been dealt, don't we?"

"We do." Sally followed him into a very dated living room. In the corner, switched on, was an old portable TV on a badly marked wooden table. The swirly carpet was threadbare in the heavy traffic areas. There was a gas fire sitting in the hearth that looked ancient and should be decommissioned and sitting on a scrap heap. Sally's heart sank. *What a come-down this is compared to the life of luxury he used to have.*

"Take a seat," he instructed. He sat in the easy chair closest to the fire. "Are you cold? I can put the fire on for ten minutes or so, to take the chill off the room, if you like?"

"Don't go to any trouble on our account. How are you?" Sally asked.

"I'm getting by, taking each day as it comes. Life can deal us a vicious blow when we least expect it."

"Apparently so. What about your family?"

His eyes watered. "It's hard. My whole life changed the day my home and my business were taken from me."

Sally picked up that he had avoided her question and decided not to push it. "We've been reading up on your case and we've been horrified by what we've learnt."

The front door opened and slammed shut seconds later. Sally and Lorne stared at each other and frowned. Not long after, two teenagers popped their heads into the lounge.

"What's for dinner?" the girl asked.

Actually, it came across as more of a demand to Sally's untrained ear.

"Beans on toast," Tim replied.

"Again!" the kids said in unison and stomped out of the room and up the stairs.

"Take your shoes off before you go up there," Tim shouted after them.

Several thuds later, and the stomping continued on the stairs.

"Sorry about the attitude, you know what teenagers are like. They're furious because I didn't get a chance to go to the foodbank today. So, it's the same dinner as they had yesterday and the day before... I think. I can't honestly remember. All the days blur into one when you're sat here with nothing else to occupy your mind."

"There's no need to apologise. I take it you don't work?" Sally asked.

"Nope. Because of what happened and it being shouted about in the newspapers, no bugger will employ me. Not that I'm in the right frame of mind to work these days. I'm under the doctor with depression. Some mornings I only get out of bed to care for the children. I sometimes think they'd be better off without me..."

Sally's eyes filled with tears. "Aww... don't say that, Tim, they need you as much as you need them."

"I know. It's their needs that I find myself considering most days, more than my own. Life sucks, it has for a long time. Still, enough about me, you haven't come here to listen to my tales of woe."

Sally ran her fingers along the flap of the envelope she'd brought with her. "I received an anonymous tip-off about a possible crime scene a few days ago..."

He uncrossed his ankles and sat forward on the edge of his seat. "And you think this has something to do with my case? In all honesty, I thought you lot had pushed it aside and were no longer working on it. It's been years since I've had any form of contact with anyone, you know, after Addis snuffed it. Sorry, that was rude of me, after he committed suicide."

145

"I apologise if that's the way you've been dealt with. What I should have explained from the outset was that we're from the Cold Case Team. I'm the officer in charge."

He ran a hand around his face. "Oh God, have you found her? Have you found my wife, Amanda?"

Sally raised her hand. "What I need you to do is see if you can identify a couple of items of jewellery we found at a crime scene."

He stared at the envelope and nodded. "I'll do my best. Let me see."

Sally withdrew the photos and handed them to him. She watched his reaction. At first, he frowned and changed the angle of the photos to get a better view, and then his expression altered to one of recognition.

He glanced up. His mouth gaped open, and he nodded. Eventually, he whispered, "I think they belonged to her."

"We thought so. The inscription in the wedding ring is what has brought us to your door. Well, that and the photo of you and your children in the locket. We compared those to the article we found in the archives, which highlighted your case."

"I understand. Is she alive? Amanda, is she coming home to us? What state is she in, after all these years?"

Sally swallowed down the bile scorching her throat. "As I said before, I received a call telling me to go to a certain address in Acle. When we showed up there, we inspected the house with SOCO and the pathologist. After a while, we discovered the jewellery, along with what we believe to be your wife's remains behind a wall in the main bedroom."

"Noooooo!" Tim shouted.

A loud thud sounded overhead followed by thundering on the stairs. Soon, the two children barged into the room.

"Dad, what is it?" the boy said.

Tim reached out his arms, and the kids tentatively walked

towards him. He hugged them tightly, almost suffocating them. The children seemed confused, their arms pinned by their sides during the hug.

"Dad, you can't keep this from us. Is it, Mum?" the boy asked.

Tim rose to his feet and looked down at his kids. "Yes, they've found her. After all this time we can finally lay your mother to rest."

"What?" the girl shouted. "Are you telling us that... she's dead?"

Tim retook his seat, his arms dropping, freeing his children. They remained glued to the spot. "Yes, but that's okay, we expected it, didn't we, kids? Now we know that she's gone to a better place. It's been a nightmare, the not knowing."

"What? How can you say that, Dad?" the girl yelled, her face bright red.

Sally couldn't blame her either. She thought Tim was dealing with the news in totally the wrong way, but everyone dealt with grief differently. Maybe this was Tim's way of coping with his loss.

"Cally, she's gone. We have to accept it," Tim said. "She's never coming back to us. This means we can now get on with our lives. Relocate to a different area, if we want to, once we've buried her, of course."

The two kids shot a glance at each other, and Cally turned her back on her father.

"You're unbelievable. All these years you've insisted that Mum was going to come back to us. We've clung on to that hope of maybe seeing her, being with her again one day, and now, you're telling us that she's gone... *forever*."

"Cally, don't turn your back on me, love, please. You have to understand, it was important for me to believe that she was still alive. We've all suffered immeasurable damage since… the day she went missing."

"We were there as well, Dad," the boy said. He threw an arm around his sister's shoulders.

"Lester, I know that. Oh God, I'm struggling here. I know what I want to say but can't seem to find the proper words, or at least put them into a sentence that makes sense. Shit! What the heck. I can't keep apologising, kids. We've been over this a million times. I'm not to blame for what happened. None of this was my fault."

Cally spun around to face him and said through gritted teeth, "Tell us whose fault it was then, if not yours. I've had enough of this, of you, of this *shitty life*. Put me in a foster home, I'm sure I'll be better off in one of them. I've had it with you." She stormed out of the room.

Her brother remained, seemingly anchored to the spot, shell-shocked by his sister's outburst.

Tim held out a hand to his son. "Lester, I couldn't bear it if either of you deserted me now, not after all we've been through."

Lester shrugged his father's arm off. "Don't, Dad. We've been to hell and back, none of it was our fault. You have no idea what she went through back then. I was with her, you weren't. I was the one whose heart was breaking while I held her at night when she cried herself to sleep after hearing those men raping Mum in the other room. She lay there, wondering when it was going to be her turn. They did untold damage to her mind, she's had to live through that nightmare for years, and now we're going to be forced to relive it all over again. We've both had enough. Maybe Cally is right. We deserve so much better than this. Look around you, Dad, we've got nothing. You can't even get off your backside, get out there and find a job."

"But, son, believe me, I've tried. It's not easy, not these days."

"That's bullshit. And no, I won't apologise for swearing in front of these ladies, I'm sure they've heard far worse from kids of my age. You need to start putting us first for a change and stop wallowing in self-pity. Our lives have become pitiful, and it's all down to you. Other men deal with bankruptcy all the time. They refuse to give in to people looking down their noses at them, demeaning them, and they get on with their lives for the sake of their families. If you're unable to cope with us then you need to do what's right for us, let us go. Let us have a chance at some sort of life, instead of letting us sink to yet another soul-destroying level. There's only so much we can take, Dad, and believe me, we've reached our limit. Actually, we met it a long time ago. You've been so wrapped up in yourself that you've neglected to see it," Lester fired at him and left the room.

Sally didn't know what to say for the best. If she spoke now, she would seem like she was intruding in the family's personal space. Didn't every family fall out once in a blue moon? Although, looking at the situation as an outsider, this felt like so much more than a simple disagreement between a father and his kids.

Tim sat in his chair, covered his face and openly sobbed in front of them. It was hard to tell if it was because of the fall out he'd had with his kids or because Sally had just delivered the devastating news that his wife's body had been discovered.

"I'll make him a drink," Lorne mouthed.

"Good idea," Sally mouthed back. "My partner's going to make you a drink, Tim. Would you like tea or coffee?"

He dropped his hands and glared at her. "Neither. We can't afford such luxuries. The kids are right, they'd be better off without me around."

Sally wagged her finger. "No, you mustn't say, or even think that. I know they're upset right now. We have to accept that hearing the news about their mother must have come as a great shock to them, but they'll calm down soon, I'm sure."

"They won't. You don't understand; that outburst has been brewing for years. I thought I'd prepared myself for this day, but clearly, I was wrong. My heart is broken all over again. The pain and misery my family have lived through is nothing compared to what lies ahead of us. We've always clung to the fact that she might be out there somewhere, biding her time to come back to us, only to be told this... all that hope has evaporated at the click of my fingers. We have nothing left. Correction, I have nothing else to give my kids, so why shouldn't I end it all?"

"We can get you some counselling to get you through the emotional upheaval you are going to have to deal with over the coming weeks, months maybe."

"We've had it with counsellors, they do fuck all good. All they do is keep going over and over the facts, never letting them remain buried in our minds. Hence, we've all had numerous nightmares over the years, especially the kids after what they had to contend with."

"Please, we want to try and help, if you'll allow us to, don't shut us out. We're willing to ease your pain, to get you through this tough time."

"How can you? If I can't see any way out of this shit? Yes, you've found her body, but what does that really mean?"

"It means that we're going to have to reopen the case. I want to assure you, my team and I don't take our work lightly. DS Warner here has dozens of years of service behind her, working in one of the toughest Forces, and areas, in the UK. London. I'm sure she won't mind me telling you that she's already retired once, but she's returned to the Force, the main reason being that she felt she had unfinished business to attend to. She's one of the best." Sally glanced at Lorne and noticed the colour rising up her neck and settling in her cheeks.

"And you're keen on embarrassing me," Lorne said. "That aside, Tim, what I think my boss is trying to say is that we have experience on our side. Over the last few years, this team, mostly before I joined them, I hasten to add, have successfully solved cold case after cold case. Investigations that have lain dormant, unforgotten for years, and even released a few prisoners who were hit with wrongful convictions, as well. They're the ultimate professionals, we all are, leaving no stone unturned. We promise you, we will find out the truth about what happened to your wife."

Sally smiled at Lorne. "I couldn't have put it better myself. Are you willing to give us a go?"

Tim stared at a threadbare patch in the carpet close to his shoeless feet, his little toe poking through the fabric of his worn-out socks. "You lot had your chance at the time, and look how that turned out. What we went through, as a family —no, correction, not me per se—but what my kids went through was utterly horrendous, and you lot couldn't have cared less about them. You didn't come close to finding them for months, until..."

Sally frowned. "Go on. I'm sorry, but we're unfamiliar with how the case concluded, how your kids came home to you. Can you perhaps fill in the blanks for us? Only if you're up to it, of course."

He reached for a glass of water sitting on the floor beside his chair, hooked out a dead fly and drank from the glass, making both Sally and Lorne shudder.

Lorne leapt out of her chair. "Why don't I refill that for you?"

Tim handed her the glass. "You'll need to run the tap.

There's that much shit in the pipes the water is brown at first, but it runs clear after a while."

Lorne left the room.

How Sally prevented herself from throwing up, she'd never know. "How long have you and the kids lived here?"

"Too long," Tim said without having to think about it. "Two years, I believe, give or take. I appear to have lost track of time over the years. Everything has become such a blur. My life, our lives, have become... well, deplorable, and that's putting it mildly. This place is still a palace compared to what some families are forced to live with these days, if watching the news is anything to go by. Landlords get a fair whack from me, okay, not me directly, but from the government through the benefit system, and this is the result. They take the money and never even check the homes are habitable. Most landlords are the same. They never think of updating the properties they rent out, and yet if you showed up at their gaffs, I bet they're all living in the lap of luxury. Life sucks for the majority of people in my situation, and the only blessed release would be if I put the kids in care and took my own life. What the fuck have I got to live for now... now that Amanda is dead?"

"First of all, I have to say, we're assuming the body belongs to your wife, only because the jewellery was found lying beside the remains."

"So, what you're saying is that I need to hang on to the little hope I've had over the years for a while longer?"

"Perhaps, for a few more days at least. I would, if I were in your shoes," she said, thinking on her feet, especially as Tim had mentioned ending his life a few times during their conversation. She couldn't bear the thought of having that on her conscience. She was determined to help this family, in any way possible. God knows they needed it.

Lorne returned and gave Tim the fresh glass of water.

"Thanks. Are you telling me you might have made a mistake?" Tim asked.

Lorne frowned and retook her seat.

Sally explained, "I'm trying to soften the blow with Tim, adding a word of caution. To tell him that until the remains have been confirmed it's always best to cling to the hope that Amanda might still be out there."

"Yes, absolutely. I totally agree," Lorne said.

"If that's the case, why come here today and disrupt me and my family like this?"

"I'm sorry if that's what you think. We needed the jewellery to be identified first and foremost, and you've kindly been able to do that for us today." She paused to consider her choice of words next. Avoiding the issue, she asked, "Can you go back, tell us what happened, how the kids found their way back to you?"

He took a sip of water and ran his finger around the rim of the glass. Sally could tell Lorne had scrubbed it clean before refilling it, as she would have, in the circumstances.

"It took six months in total to find them. I'd given up all hope of them ever coming back to me, then, out of the blue, Addis showed up one day and said I was to go with him. He drove me to the hospital, to the A and E Department, and that's where Cally and Lester were." He shook his head as the memories resurfaced once more.

"Take your time. Did the police get a tip-off? Did Addis put out a press conference, requesting help from the public?"

"Yes and no. He went before the cameras months earlier, when it was obvious that the kidnappers had no intention of releasing my family. I was as shocked as Addis was when the kids showed up."

"I see. What did he tell you? I don't recall seeing anything in the notes about them coming home. Granted, I only read the file briefly, eager to visit you."

"He told me one of his contacts came through for him. Someone from the underground had heard about two kids being put up for auction in the slave trade."

"What? In this country or abroad?"

Tim inhaled a shuddering breath. "Yes, although Cally and Lester were part of a group of kids who had been snatched off the streets and were being held in a warehouse, waiting to be transferred to one of the Arab countries, not sure which one. I was so relieved to have them back home with me, I let things drop. I know I shouldn't have, but knowing they were missing for six months, well... you can't begin to imagine what that does to a person. What those kids went through... it must have been soul-destroying for them."

"I bet. I'm sorry if reliving this is upsetting for you, but it's important we hear all the facts if we're going to find the people responsible for ruining your lives."

"Do you think you'll ever find them? It's been five years. Won't they have buggered off to another country long ago? Surely, they wouldn't have hung around, would they?"

"I can't answer that, not until we start digging. Do you know what happened with Addis?"

"No, not really. He took me to the hospital to visit the children, and then I never really saw him again after that. Warren, the officer who remained with me when I got out of hospital, dropped by a few days later and told me that Addis had ended his life. I couldn't understand it, he always seemed such a strong-willed character to me. I suppose we never really know people well enough to know what's going on in their heads, do we?"

"I suppose. Maybe the strain of the case proved to be too much for him in the end. Again, we'll have to check back on our database, to find out what actually happened. The main thing is that your kids were safely returned to you."

He stared at Sally and exhaled a deep sigh. "At what cost?"

He peered over his shoulder before he spoke again. "They've never been the same since, either of them, particularly Cally. She went into her shell, refused to speak to me for a couple of years. We went through half a dozen counsellors. I know earlier I told you they've all been shit, but I wasn't really telling you the truth. We struck gold with Michele, the last one on the list for us to try. She was compassionate and understanding, always allowed Cally the time to get to know her, never forced her to open up to her. Eventually, that's what Cally did, opened up to her, revealed all that she had been through. It was horrific. Lester, if I can say this, he got off lightly compared to his sister. She literally went to Hell and back."

Sally faced Lorne. Her eyes were bulging with tears, obviously still haunted by what Charlie had been through at the hands of her nemesis, The Unicorn, when Charlie had only been thirteen. Sally touched her partner's leg, jolting her out of her reverie. Lorne smiled and nodded, reassuring her that she was okay.

"What's going on?" Tim asked.

Sally didn't say anything. She left it up to Lorne to reveal the truth, if she felt the need to.

"It's okay, I personally understand what you and Cally went through."

"How could you?" he snapped back as if Lorne had offended him.

"Because my daughter was kidnapped when she was thirteen. She was treated... like a sex slave by a notorious gangster I was dealing with back in London."

"Shit, I'm sorry. I didn't mean to snap at you. Can I ask you how you and your daughter coped with the ordeal?"

Lorne wiped her eyes on her sleeve and smiled at him. "It wasn't easy. We both had to be patient and work through our emotions, one day at a time. My daughter has a strong spirit.

She refused to let the bastard win, to destroy her life, even after his death."

"What? He died?"

"Umm… yes, that's a story best left for another time. All you need to know is there is life after being involved in such a heinous crime, but it takes time and understanding. Is Cally still seeing Michele?"

"Yes, after all these years that woman has stuck by her. You can see the way my daughter had a go at me earlier, she has her mother's lioness spirit. Although it has taken her a couple of years to get to this stage. Lord knows how much this news is going to set her back now. She already loathes me."

Sally took over the conversation once more. "I'm sure she doesn't. I can tell that's not the case, just watching her inter-action with you."

"Maybe, but you've only got to see what the kids have to put up with, to know what a strain that has put on our rela-tionship over the years, especially lately, as the kids get older and are finding their feet in the world."

"They seem pretty confident to me," Sally noted.

"Confident? I suppose that's true of Lester, he's coming up to sixteen now." He took another peek over his shoulder and added quietly. "Last year he got involved with a gang and… let's just say it has not all been plain sailing with him. Things have been tense between us in recent weeks. However, he's continued to do well at school and, while his grades maintain the level they've always been, who am I to question what he does after school?"

"It's better to keep a watchful eye on him, though. Kids can be easily influenced at his age, just be aware of that."

"I will. Not that I can do a lot to stop him. He's getting to the stage where he's trying to parent me, if you get my drift?"

They all laughed.

"Stay strong and determined with him. I know that's not easy after what you've been through, however, teenagers need a lot of guidance."

"You're not kidding. I'm doing my best."

"Talking about counsellors, have you ever gone down that route?"

"No, it has never occurred to me." His head dipped.

Sally got the impression that he was possibly telling a white lie. "Come now, if you've seen the effect this Michele has had on Cally, wouldn't it be worth you giving it a shot? Unless, of course, there's a reason why you wouldn't want to feel better about yourself?" Sally sensed there might be an underlying issue at play.

"If I 'get cured' as it were, then that means I will no longer need to live with the guilt. I was to blame for all the disastrous things that happened to my family."

"How were you to blame?" Sally challenged.

He hitched up a shoulder and avoided eye contact with her.

"Did you know who the kidnappers were?" Sally asked.

"No, it never came out, which is the frustrating part. I've spent the last five years contemplating how it all developed."

"And what conclusions have you drawn from all you've put yourself through?"

He glanced up and grinned at her. "Nothing. I keep drawing a massive blank."

Sally held her palms up. "There you have it, you need to stop punishing yourself and get on with your life, not only for your sake but you also have the kids to consider, too. What about your family? Have they been there for you over the years?"

"My parents both died in a train crash when I was a teenager."

"I'm sorry to hear that. Do you have any siblings?"

"No. I was an only child, which I preferred in my younger days as I was the one receiving all my parents' love and attention. I had an incredibly happy childhood. It was something I was desperate to achieve for my own kids. That kind of blew up in my face, didn't it? I feel as though I've let not only the kids down but my deceased parents as well."

"What utter nonsense that is," Sally reprimanded him harshly, maybe a little too much, judging by the shock on his face. "I'm sorry, I shouldn't have said that."

"Is it, though? What's a parent's primary job, if not to protect their child?"

Lorne tutted. "I have to admit, I went through the same emotional turmoil back in the day, but as soon as my daughter was home safe and well, we managed to set those thoughts aside. We were able to sit down and talk to each other. I know this probably sounds silly, but Charlie getting kidnapped revitalised our relationship. It was getting worse by the day, and suddenly, it flipped on its head. We're closer now than we've ever been."

"Lucky you. The exact opposite happened to me and Cally, and honestly, I can't see a way back from it now, not after all this time."

"Never say never," Lorne said. "I can tell she loves you very much. Obviously, the situation you find yourself in isn't ideal, but don't give up, that would be my advice. Do they have maternal grandparents and other members of the family?"

"Yes. Their grandparents have always been distant with the kids. I could understand them having gripes with me, but not the children. Don't get me wrong, they haven't disowned them, nothing like that, just... well, kept their distance more than I expected them to."

"That's sad," Sally said. "Talking of which, I'm going to

need their names and address, we're going to need to break the news to them about Amanda."

"What? Now? Or will you wait until you receive formal identification, bearing in mind what you told me earlier?"

"We'll pay them a visit after we leave here, tell them the same thing we've told you. It would be wrong of me to keep them in the dark and I wouldn't want any backlash from them if they discovered the truth."

"Ah, yes. I'm guessing the kids won't be able to keep it a secret for long."

"Are they due to visit their grandparents soon?" Sally asked.

"Not to my knowledge. They tend to pick them up and put them down when it suits them. Let's put it this way, they never come here to see them, they would never lower themselves that much. Let me find you their address and phone number." He left his seat and the room. He was gone a while.

"What do you make of him?" Lorne whispered.

"Hard to tell. I'm on the fence. We'll discuss it when we're in the car," Sally rushed at the end, hearing him in the hallway, cussing under his breath. "Any luck?" she called out.

"I thought the address book was in the kitchen but now I can't find it. I'm going upstairs. I'll see if the kids can give me the details. I won't be long."

"Take your time."

"I mean, I feel sorry for him, I wasn't being disrespectful," Lorne said as if clarifying what she'd said previously.

"I know. I suppose we need to consider what they've been through as a family and how we would be likely to act." Sally winced. "Shit! Me and my big mouth. Forget I said that."

Lorne chuckled. "It's forgotten. He's a broken man. I wish there was something we could do for him to get him out of the hole he's in."

"Like what? That's not our responsibility, Lorne. This

159

type of thing happens all the time. It's up to the people concerned to bounce back. You and Charlie both came through the experience relatively unaffected, didn't you?"

"I wouldn't quite put it that way, but compared to others, yes, we came out of our personal nightmare relatively unscathed."

The conversation died between them, and Tim returned to the room a few seconds later.

"Here it is, Cally gave it to me." He handed Sally a page from a small notebook.

"That's fantastic, thanks very much. Sorry, I should have said before you went off on your hunt. We're going to need something to possibly obtain DNA from, a hairbrush perhaps. Did Amanda have one that only she used?"

"I can't help you there. I got rid of most of her personal belongings, things of that nature, when we moved. Although, I did bring a few suitcases of clothes with us… just in case she ever came back. Will they be of use?"

"Not really. Maybe you can tell us who your family dentist was at the time she went missing?"

"That's easy enough. I haven't registered with another dentist since we moved. The kids have, I made sure they were covered, but I really can't be arsed with things like that, not many dentists are taking on NHS patients these days. I did try a couple in this area when we first moved in but stopped trying after the first few told me to bugger off. The Whole Tooth Practice in Wymondham. I believe it's not far from the police station."

"I know the one," Lorne was quick to add.

"That's perfect then. Okay, we're going to leave it there for today. I think we've put you through enough for one day. We'll get the ball rolling on the investigation now, chase up a few people we feel we need to have a chat with and will hopefully get back to you with the PM results soon. Do you have a phone number I can contact you on?"

He shook his head. "Nope, I can't afford the monthly contract. A phone is a luxury in this house, rather than a necessity."

"I understand." Sally rose to her feet.

Lorne and Tim followed suit, and the three of them walked into the hallway to the front door where Sally and Lorne shook Tim's hand.

"I want to assure you that we're going to do our utmost to find out what happened to your wife, Tim."

"I hope you don't let me and, more importantly, my kids down. They deserve better, they always have done. I've had to live through five years of frustration and, to be honest, now you've broken the news to us, I'm not sure what lies ahead for any of us."

"It's a tough time for you, and them. All I can say is, perhaps continue as you are for now. Take each day as it comes until you receive a positive ID from us and go from there. In the meantime, we'll be working our socks off to find out why your family was targeted in the first place. If we can source the truth, the next step will be to find the kidnappers and arrest them."

Tim crossed his fingers and held them up. "I want that more than anything, especially now, if indeed the remains do belong to Amanda." He shook his head. "I can't believe she's gone. I know she's been missing for five years but... this seems so final now. As if I have to go through the torment of losing her all over again. Lord knows how this is going to affect the children."

"Try and get your own feelings in order first before you start tackling Cally's and Lester's. Wait, maybe it would be advantageous to let the counsellor know, prewarn her if Cally is due to visit her soon."

"Worth considering. I'll see if she can have a word with Lester as well. Thanks for the suggestion and for coming to visit me in person. I know the news was unexpected, but was it really? I suppose I've been waiting for this day to come for years."

"Hopefully, it will ease your mind a little, even though we haven't got a full positive ID as yet."

"I might be able to sleep better tonight, I can't say I've had that much over the years. Or perhaps the opposite will be true, and I'll be far worse knowing, reliving the events of when the kidnappings occurred and living with the recriminations I went through at the time."

"I'm not saying it's going to be easy for any of you, but I will say one thing, don't ever think you're alone, not with me and DS Warner on the case. We tend to put the families we're dealing with first." She gave him one of her cards.

Tim took it and held out his arms. "Is it the done thing to give you a hug?"

Sally smiled. "I have no objections."

He tugged her into a firm embrace. When they parted again there were tears in Tim's eyes.

"Why couldn't you have been around back then? I feel confident about you working the case. I never felt that with Addis, ever. It's probably wrong of me to say this, but at times, I was made to feel like I was a bloody criminal. As if he blamed me for my family being kidnapped. I'll tell you one thing, he couldn't have blamed me more than I did myself."

"That part of it is over now. It's time to move on with your life. Time for you to become a family once more. You're going to need to help each other through one of the toughest times ahead of you."

"I think the kids will come around. I'll leave them for now. I think they'll have a lot of soul-searching to carry out this evening. We'll begin to pick up the threads of our lives tomorrow and try to move forward, as a family."

Sally smiled. "That's the spirit. With our help, you've got this, Tim."

"I hope so. Thank you, to both of you."

Neither Sally nor Lorne spoke until they were settled in the car. Sally turned right at the end of the road. She pulled into the nearest parking space and applied the handbrake.

"I'm sorry, I need to take a breather for a moment or two. I'm an emotional wreck."

Lorne sighed. "Hey, don't be too hard on yourself, that goes for me, too. It's never easy breaking this type of news to a loved one. The fact that we couldn't give him a definitive answer at this time doesn't sit comfortably with me, either. We need to prepare ourselves for much of the same when we visit her parents."

Sally groaned. "Yeah, maybe that's why I needed the break." She shook out her arms and eased her head over to the right and then the left, to relieve the tension in her neck. "All sorted and ready for the next round. I hope they're gentle on us."

Lorne chuckled. "In your dreams. I wouldn't count on it, not after being left high and dry by our predecessors. We should be used to people taking other coppers' failings out on us by now, though, shouldn't we?"

"Totally true. Have I mentioned lately how much I loathe this job?"

"Not recently, no. We all despise our jobs now and again, but then we must look at the positive side of our work."

"Care to remind me what that is? I'm struggling at this time to put my finger on it."

"Bollocks. Stop winding me up. Consider this, if you will. What type of people would we be if this didn't mess with our heads now and then?"

Sally indicated and left her parking space. "You're a wise woman, Lorne Warner. Too wise for your own good sometimes."

Lorne frowned. "What's that supposed to mean?"

Sally shrugged. "I'll let you know when I find out."

They both laughed.

CHAPTER 10

*T*he Tylers lived in a modest detached house on a newish estate on the outskirts of Watton, not too far from the location where Sally and Lorne had solved their last case.

"Seems strange being back here again so soon," Sally said.

"I was just thinking the same. I wonder how the family are getting on."

"I'm going to try not to dwell on that one. It was a heart-breaking case to deal with, wasn't it?"

"Let's face it, they all are."

"You have a point. Okay, brace yourself for another emotional onslaught."

They got out of the car, and Lorne replied, "I'm prepared. Hey, they might surprise us and be totally chilled by it all."

Sally cocked an eyebrow and pressed her key fob to lock the doors. "And pigs might fly."

Lorne glanced up at the black clouds above. "Maybe on a clear day."

"Shut up. We're supposed to have our serious heads on. Hopefully we can make this a quick visit and get back to the station ASAP. There's plenty for us to action once we get back."

"Wouldn't you rather take two minutes out to get that organised, delay this visit for a while?"

"I would, but my conscience won't allow me to do it. These people deserve to know the truth. It wouldn't be right to tell the husband and not her parents."

"You're right, of course. It was just a thought. Let's hope we don't have to hang around here for too long."

"We'll see how that pans out, eh?"

Sally led the way up the open front garden. There were postage stamps of a lawn on either side of the front door, which had a few shrubs strategically placed under each of the windows. "Nice enough, bog-standard design from the house builders, I shouldn't wonder."

"Yeah, you're not wrong. Some of the other houses across the road have embellished theirs a little."

"Get you. Right, here goes." Sally rang the bell.

The door was opened by a grey-haired gentleman wearing a plaid shirt and brown corduroy trousers. "Yes, can I help?"

Sally held up her ID. "DI Sally Parker and DS Lorne Warner from the Cold Case Team based in Wymondham, Mr Tyler. Is it possible to come in and speak with you and your wife?"

The colour drained from his face, and he whispered, "You've found her, haven't you?"

"It would be better if we come inside and explained the situation to you, sir, if you don't mind?"

He took a step back and called over his shoulder for his wife, "Susie, stop what you're doing and come downstairs, please."

"But I told you I was putting away the ironing. I won't be long, Ian. Have some patience for once in your life."

"We've got visitors. Now would be preferable, love. Don't argue, please."

Stomping could be heard overhead, and then a slender woman with dyed brown hair appeared at the top of the stairs. "Who is it?"

"Come down here and I'll tell you." He closed the door after Lorne had entered the hallway. "Come through to the lounge."

Sally nodded and smiled at the lady descending the stairs.

"I'm not going to like what you have to say, am I?" she muttered as she swept past them.

Neither Sally nor Lorne answered her question. Sally inhaled a large breath to steady her pounding heart rate.

"Come in and take a seat. My wife and I will sit together on the sofa. Why don't you take the armchairs? Sorry, I should have asked, can I get you both a drink?"

"Not for us, thank you."

The four of them sat.

Sally glanced at the couple and smiled, not too keenly, just enough to try and put them at ease. "Mr and Mrs Tyler, as I've already stated, my partner and I are from the Cold Case Team."

Mrs Tyler gasped and gripped her husband's hand in both of hers. "Oh no. I knew this day would come..."

"Stop jumping to conclusions, Susie, let's see what the officer has to say first. Go on, how can we help you, Inspector?"

Before the conversation could get underway, the front door opened and a woman in her forties poked her head into the room. "Hey, I've bought the stuff you requested from the butcher's... oops, excuse me, I didn't know you had visitors coming today, you should have told me."

"This is our daughter, Jane," Mr Tyler said. "Jane, dump the bags in the kitchen and join us. These two ladies are from the police, they've only just arrived. We've got no idea what it's about, although I can probably guess."

"Oh no, the police? I'll be back in a mo."

An awkward silence filled the room until Jane entered and squeezed on the end of the couch, next to her father. "What's going on? Have either of you been involved in something dodgy and failed to mention it to me?"

"No, it's nothing like that," Sally jumped in. "Unfortunately, I have some bad news for you all, but it comes with a word of caution."

"What? That doesn't make sense. What are you on about?" Jane demanded.

"I recently received a call from a person instructing me to go to an address in Acle. Presuming it was a crime scene," Sally chose her words cautiously, "we notified SOCO and the pathologist to meet us at the location."

"Oh no… don't tell us you've found her?" Jane said.

She clutched her parents' hands, and the three of them stared expectantly at Sally.

"I'm sorry, a body was found at the property, or should I say, the remains of a person. I need to add a warning here. We won't be able to confirm a formal ID until the postmortem has been completed. What I can tell you is that two pieces of jewellery were found close to the remains. These have already been identified as your daughter's."

"Who by? Was it him?" Mrs Tyler snapped.

"If you mean Tim, then yes. We've just come from visiting him, and he was the one who confirmed they belonged to Amanda."

Mrs Tyler closed her eyes, and the tears rolled down her cheeks. Mr Tyler and Jane both stared at each other and shook their heads.

"When will we know for sure?" Jane asked after the news had time to sink in.

"We've been given the name of your sister's dentist. We're going to drop by there, after we leave here. Hopefully they'll supply us with the evidence we need to help the pathologist formally identify the remains."

"In the meantime, you've come here for what purpose?" Jane snarled.

"Not to upset you, I can assure you. I thought it right to come and inform your parents before they heard the news secondhand."

"From him?"

Sally nodded. "Yes, or possibly the children."

"Oh God, they know?" Mrs Tyler asked. Fresh tears emerged and dripped onto her cheek.

"Yes, they arrived home from school as we were talking to Tim. He insisted they should know right away; he didn't want to keep them in the dark."

"At least he's done something right, after all these years of bringing those kids up. Poor buggers, living in a shithole like that."

"I don't want to get into the rights and wrongs of where they live. I believe Tim has done the best for his children in very trying circumstances over the years." Sally felt the need to defend Tim against the three people sitting in front of her, perhaps a little too fiercely, judging by their shocked expressions.

"And you've come to that conclusion from a brief visit you've had with him today, have you?" Jane asked.

"Yes, we spent about an hour with him. In my defence, I have always regarded myself as a good judge of character during my time serving as a police officer."

"No doubt able to easily suss out people who are trying to pull the wool over your eyes," Jane challenged.

Sally sensed a battle of wills coming up. "I like to think so, yes. If you've got something to say, Jane, you should just come out and say it."

"Don't worry, I have plenty to say on the matter. Are you going to take notes?"

Without prompting, Lorne withdrew her notebook and pen from her pocket.

"Of course. Are you about to tell us something significant about the kidnapping that you neglected to tell the officer in charge of the case at the time your sister and her kids were abducted?" Sally called the woman's bluff, sensing Jane was about to unleash a tirade of abuse about Tim.

"Go easy, my girl," Mr Tyler cautioned his daughter.

"Don't you start. You should have done more to get those kids away from that man. He doesn't deserve to be their legal guardian after what he's put them through."

"Why do you believe that, Jane?" Sally asked.

"What? I can't believe you would ask such a stupid question after coming from there."

"What we saw was a desperate man trying to look after his children with the odds stacked against him. He has no living relatives he can rely on to assist him. I should imagine bringing up two teenagers alone is no easy task. Tell me, when was the last time you saw or even spoke to your niece and nephew?"

"I… umm… it was last Christmas, I think."

Sally rolled her eyes. "That would be eleven months ago. Have you even offered to look after those children overnight in the last five years, since your sister went missing?"

Jane had the decency to drop her head in shame.

"Enough of this." Mrs Tyler threw an arm around her daughter's shoulder and pulled her close. "We're not the ones at fault here."

"I can speak for myself, Mum. I don't need you to fight my battles, I never have done, unlike Amanda."

"Jane! Stop it before you say something you might regret," her father warned.

"No, it needs to be aired, I've been dying to get this off my chest... I've bottled it up for years. She was always the apple of your eyes, both of you. Most of the time I felt like a spare part in this family. Not any more. I intend to say my piece, and you're going to listen."

"Now isn't the right time or place to air your family grievances. Stop being selfish for once in your life," Mr Tyler chastised her.

"Selfish? Me? Are you crazy? I've had enough of this." Jane stormed out of the room.

Sally glanced at Lorne, torn about what to do next. "Umm... do you need to be with her? We can come back and finish off our conversation another time if you need to sort out this family drama."

"There's always a drama in the offing where Jane and her brother are concerned. It's been a full-time job for both of us over the years, keeping everyone happy and involved. I'm sick of it. We're retired now, this should be our time to enjoy ourselves. Instead, we're being constantly bombarded with this type of bullshit." Mr Tyler ran his hands through his hair.

His wife held out her hand for him to hold once more. He did, after a moment's hesitation.

"Don't let her get to you. We'll sort it out once and for all as soon as the officers leave."

"Will we? You're always telling me that. We should never have allowed it to have got this far in the first place. But we need to set this aside and listen to what the police have to say."

"We're in no rush if you want to see if Jane is all right before we continue."

"No, let her sulk in peace. I'd rather hear the news you have to tell us," Mr Tyler insisted.

"That's about all there is to tell you, if I'm honest. I thought you had a right to know that a discovery had been made and that the team are working through the process to bring you a swift result."

"I can't believe it, after all these years. I won't say we'd given up hope of ever finding her but… near as damn it," Mrs Tyler admitted.

"So, you're telling us that the dentist will be the key in identifying her, is that it?" Mr Tyler asked.

"Yes. I did ask Tim if he had a comb or hairbrush which belonged to Amanda, but he said he had only kept a couple of suitcases of her clothes in case she came back."

"Figures," Mr Tyler grumbled. "Are you going to divulge what the conditions were like for our daughter? Where was she found exactly?"

"Umm… we were led to believe that her body was buried at the property. SOCO found her remains tucked behind the wall in the main bedroom."

"What? It was there all that time?"

"So it would appear."

"And who owns the property?"

"Ahh… we're in the process of searching for the new owner now."

"New owner? As in it has recently been sold?" Mr Tyler asked.

"I'd rather not go into detail. At first glance it appears complicated. We haven't found out much regarding the ownership, as such, and I wouldn't want to be accused of misleading you further down the line."

The door opened again, and instead of Jane standing in the doorway, it was filled by a man in his mid-to-late thirties. Sally wondered if this was Jane and Amanda's brother.

"Jane said the police were here. Why? And why is Jane sitting in the kitchen, bawling her eyes out?" he demanded, his angry gaze flitting between his parents.

"I'll go and see if she's all right," Mrs Tyler said.

"There you go, letting her win again. When are you going to stop allowing her to walk all over you, Susie?" her husband asked, irate.

"Pack it in, Dad. Just because your heart is made of stone, it doesn't mean Mum's is. If she wants to check on Jane, her only living daughter, why shouldn't she?"

Susie stood between the two men and stamped her foot. "Grow up, the pair of you. Isn't this day hard enough as it is without all of you kicking off? Why do I have to continue to be the one who has to constantly referee this family? You're all old enough to know better, give me a frigging break once in a while."

She took a swipe at her son. He ducked out of the way.

She reached the door and said, "I'm sorry, ladies, you haven't come here to witness this shit."

"Don't worry about us, you do what you need to do, Mrs Tyler. We've both come across far worse in our time on the Force." Sally said, smiling at the distraught woman.

"They need locking up. If you have a few free cells down at the station anytime, please let me know. I could do with a few hours' peace and quiet now and again."

"Unfair, Ma," her son whined.

"Is it?" Susie slammed the door after she left the room, and it wasn't long before raised voices could be heard in the kitchen.

"Why are you here?" the son demanded. He took a few steps towards his father and then turned to face Sally and Lorne.

Sally glanced at Mr Tyler and asked, "Do you want to fill your son in?"

"Yes. Take a seat, Chris, and stop causing hassle for once in your life."

Chris opened his mouth to object, but his father pointed at the sofa and tapped his foot until Chris had taken a seat.

"These officers have been here no more than fifteen minutes and they've witnessed all of us arguing. What type of impression do you think they're going to get from that?"

"I don't give a shit, why should I?"

"Because your sister's body was discovered buried in a wall at a house, that's why."

Chris bounced to his feet once more. "What? Where? How long has she been there? Is she intact? How do they know it's her?"

"Sit down. Keep a civil tongue in your head. Please, don't answer his questions, it's my wife and I who should be told the facts first, not our children who are both intent on acting like spoilt brats, doing their best to show us up."

"Give it a rest, Dad. What the heck has got into you and Mum today? You never speak to us this way."

"Maybe that's been the problem over the years. Sit down and shut up. This conversation will not continue until my wife is back, beside me, where she should be."

The shouting intensified in the kitchen.

Mr Tyler excused himself and left the room. He bellowed two words, "Shut up!" and the shouting ceased. Moments later, Mr and Mrs Tyler and their reluctant daughter came back into the room.

"Please, continue," Mr Tyler said, giving Sally the go-ahead to pick up where she'd left off.

"Thank you. We won't take up much of your time. All we need to know is what you can tell us about the kidnapping, if anything?"

"Who is that question directed to?" a tearful Mrs Tyler asked.

"All of you. We're going to have to reopen the case again now. We're a specialist team and give every investigation we work on one hundred percent. We will get to the truth."

"Good. We need to know what happened to Amanda. The last copper working the case was worse than bloody useless," Chris said. "The only good thing he ever did was ending his own life."

Sally stared at the mouthy individual, lost for words. Thankfully, his mother stepped forward and slapped him around the face.

"What the fuc… what was that for, Ma?"

"What a thing to say. We brought you up better than that, Chris. Stop showing off, allowing your ignorance to shine through. Either that, or leave now and let the grownups have a sensible conversation."

He sank into the sofa and folded his arms in defiance but said nothing further.

"If you can think back to the time the kidnapping took place, did anything strike you as strange around then?" Sally enquired.

"Meaning what?" Jane asked. "You think someone getting kidnapped is the norm, is that what you're telling us?"

"No, I meant did anything happen before the event that possibly raised your suspicions?" Sally clarified.

"With him? Tim? Is that who you're talking about?" Mr Tyler asked.

"With either of them. Could either of them have been having an affair?"

"No way, not our Amanda," Mrs Tyler jumped in quickly. "As for him, I wouldn't like to say. He never seemed to be at home much. Amanda always dismissed any negativity I had about that at the time. She always made excuses for Tim, said he was doing his best to make the factory a success and told me to stop looking for something that wasn't there."

Sally nodded. "That's good to hear. I don't suppose you know the name of Amanda's best friend, do you?"

"Yes, that would be Milly, er, I can't for the life of me recall her surname now, can you, Jane?" Mrs Tyler said.

"Yeah, it's Rowlandson. They were friends from their school days. Milly was always at our house when we were kids."

"Thanks. Do you happen to know if she still lives in the area?"

"Yes. She owns a nail bar in Attleborough that is really busy. I doubt if she would give that up easily. I hear it has recently expanded because of how busy they got after the pandemic," Jane confirmed.

"Do you know the name of it?" Lorne asked.

"No. There can't be that many around, can there? You'll have to use your detective skills to find the right one."

"That's enough, Jane. There's no need for sarcasm," her father chastised.

Jane mumbled an apology.

"Is there anything else you can add that you feel we should look into?" Sally asked. She had a feeling she wasn't going to get any further with the family, except for the odd snipe here and there from either Jane or her brother.

The parents glanced at each other and shrugged. Jane and Chris just stared at Sally, until Chris said, "What you need to do is dig into that copper's past, the one who was supposedly meant to be working the case when he died. In my opinion, he did the bare minimum to try to find Amanda. You need to ask yourself one question, why?"

Sally inclined her head and narrowed her eyes. "Are you telling me you think he was involved in the kidnapping?"

Chris held her gaze, and his lip curled up as he spoke. "You tell me."

"Okay, then if there's nothing else, we're going to make a

move. I'll pass on your details to the pathologist. She'll get in touch with you if she has got any questions. As soon as I have the results of the post-mortem, I'll give you a ring. Hopefully, we'll be able to lay Amanda to rest soon."

"If it's her," Jane muttered and turned her back on Sally.

Sally chose to ignore the woman, and she and Lorne bid the family farewell and left the room. Mr Tyler caught up with them at the front door and apologised for the rudeness of his family.

"Please, sir, there's no need. It's understandable in the circumstances. We'll be in touch soon."

"Thank you. Please, do your very best for us. We deserve to know the truth after all this time."

"I agree, and hopefully we'll have some news for you soon. We won't let you down."

"I feel sure you won't."

LORNE RANG the dentist while Sally drove to Attleborough. The dentist agreed to have Amanda's file ready for when they passed by later that day, on the way back to the station.

"Here it is. Fabulous Nails. I hope she doesn't study mine too closely." Sally chuckled.

"Christ, yours are in far better condition than mine. Don't forget I have the dogs to deal with when I get home every night."

"You don't have to do the mucky jobs now that you've employed someone as a kennel manager, do you?"

"There's only so much cleaning et cetera she can do during the day. She tries her best. It really depends on whether she's had any visitors to the kennels during the day or not. We're at full capacity at present, plus she's also trying to arrange several money-making ideas that we've discussed. I'm happy to lend a hand when I get home. She's got a tough

177

job, and I would never want to take her for granted and end up losing her."

"You're an enigma, Lorne Warner. There, I've often thought it, but I've finally voiced my opinion. You're amazing, there's no doubt about it. And those dogs are lucky they have you fighting their corner."

Lorne waved away the sudden praise. "Nonsense. We're the lucky ones. They're all very special and they deserve the best homes available. We try to source that for them. Not everyone who shows an interest in one of our dogs is successful. Abby has a rigorous checklist she goes through before she allows someone to take one of the dogs home with them. Plus, we don't charge exorbitant adoption fees like some of these places. Granted, they've got a lot of staff to fund, unlike us, but I think it's off-putting how some rescue centres charge between five and six hundred pounds for an adoption fee."

"Are you kidding me? That's terrible."

"Yep. We ensure the dogs are happy with their new owners for the first three months, as well. If they're not, we take them back."

"Blimey, you kept that under your hat. I bet you and Tony both fund that place out of your salaries then, am I right?"

"All the time. Honestly, I wouldn't have it any other way. We're doing what's right for the dogs. Enough about me and the pooches, we're here to see Milly. Let's hope she's more willing to talk to us than Amanda's family were."

"We can but hope. Hey, if ever you're short of funds, I can always make a donation, or we could set up a regular donation through Simon's business, if it will help."

Lorne laughed. "Hadn't you better run that past Simon before you suggest it?"

"Oops, maybe I should. I'll have a word later. He'll agree, I'm sure he will."

They exited the car, and Sally walked into the nail bar first. It was exceptionally busy with lots of staff. There were customers at every workstation and a couple of them waiting to be seen, either flicking through a magazine or scrolling through their phones.

A woman in her early forties with dyed red hair approached them. "Hello, do you have an appointment, or is this just an enquiry?"

"The latter." Sally produced her warrant card. "We'd like to have a chat with Milly if she's available. I'm DI Sally Parker, and this is my partner, DS Lorne Warner."

"I'm Milly. Have we done something wrong?"

"Is there somewhere private we can have a chat?"

"Yes, my office. Come this way." She turned and headed towards the rear of the shop. She stopped briefly to whisper something in one of her colleague's ears and then continued on her journey. Once in the large office, Milly gestured for them to take a seat. "What's this about?"

"We're investigating the kidnapping of…"

"Amanda? After all this time. Why?" Milly interrupted.

"New evidence has come to light."

"What new evidence? Do you know who has her? Has someone seen her and reported the sighting to you guys? Is that what you're telling me?" Milly asked excitedly.

Sally raised a hand. "If you'll let me finish. The last thing I want to do is get your hopes up."

"My hopes up? But you just said someone had seen her. What's going on here?"

"No, what I said was that new evidence has come our way. I'm sorry to be the bearer of bad news, but remains have been discovered, and there's every indication it might be Amanda."

Milly gasped and poured herself a glass of water from the bottle she removed from the drawer beside her. "I can't get my head around this. Are you telling me she's dead and after all this time her body has shown up out of the blue?"

"Let me see if I can make it clearer for you. I received a call telling me that a body could be found at an address in Acle. Hours later, the discovery was made."

"What condition is the body in, bearing in mind she's been missing for five years?"

"Not good. We're going to need access to her dental records to help make a formal ID."

"Forgive my confusion, but why are you here if you haven't identified her yet?"

"Sorry, I was getting around to telling you that two pieces of jewellery were discovered alongside the body, and her husband has confirmed they belonged to Amanda."

Milly's gaze drifted to the other side of the room. Sally looked that way and spotted a picture of Milly with another woman who she recognised as Amanda. Sally faced Milly again.

"I'm sorry the news couldn't be better."

"It's okay. I think I knew years ago that she was dead. People just don't disappear like that and never return, do they? I know she was kidnapped, but even then, after Tim finding all that money for the ransom, they still refused to let her go. What type of sick individual would do that kind of thing? And why is it up to you to reopen the investigation?"

"It's procedure when a body has been discovered. We've visited Tim and Amanda's family and asked them if they can give us anything new to go on in order for us to make a fresh start with the investigation. They couldn't. I wanted to see you in the hope that Amanda might have confided in you more, what with you being her best friend. Can you help us?"

"What would I know? If you're asking me who I think the kidnappers were, I haven't got a clue. Wouldn't know where to begin either."

"Putting aside the kidnapping for a while, perhaps you can give us an insight into what state their marriage was in before Amanda went missing?"

"State their marriage was in? Do you think this was down to Tim?"

Sally vehemently shook her head. "No, that's not what I was insinuating at all. I'm going to come right out and say it."

"I wish you would." Milly's frown gave way to a broad grin.

"Did Amanda confide in you, perhaps intimate that either of them was having an affair?"

"We confided in each other all the time. She was closer to me than she was to her sister, Jane. She's an odd one."

"In what way?" Sally asked, interested to hear what someone else's take was on the woman who had got her back up not half an hour since.

"Both of them are a bit weird, she and her brother. They weren't that close, not really."

"Are you telling us there was animosity between the siblings?"

"Animosity? Not sure if that's the word. All I know is they were both extremely jealous of Amanda and Tim's success. I was thrilled with it; they were a delightful family. Tim was a workaholic, that pissed Amanda off here and there. In the end she realised he was only doing it to give them and the kids a better future."

Her gaze drifted again, and Sally was determined not to let the moment pass.

"Did Amanda feel neglected at times?"

"Yes, that's exactly how I would put it."

"Enough to start an affair with someone?"

Milly sighed. "No, it never went that far."

Lorne nudged Sally's knee under the desk. "How far did it go? And with whom?"

Milly licked her lips and ran her tongue around her teeth. "I don't know. She mentioned she'd been flirting with a bloke. At first, I encouraged her. I know it was foolish of me, but at the time I felt she deserved to be treated better by her husband."

"Who was the man?"

"His name was Dave Clark, if that was his real name."

"Why do you say that?" Sally asked.

"Because after a few weeks she revealed the truth about him."

"Which was?" *Bloody hell, get on with it, woman.*

"That her dalliance, if you can call it that, was with… with an ex-con. She finally broke down and told me that he'd been inside numerous times."

Lorne scribbled down the information.

Sally rested her hand on Lorne's arm. "Get on the phone to the station, Lorne, see what the team can find out about this man."

Lorne left the room to make the call.

"What if I'm wrong? What if he finds out I've mentioned his name to the police, and he comes after me?"

Sally noticed Milly's hand trembling and the water sloshing around in the glass.

"Don't worry, I'm sure that won't happen. DI Addis originally investigated the case. Did you make him aware of this dalliance between them?"

"He wasn't interested. You've asked more questions in the five minutes you've been here than he ever asked me."

"I'm sorry to hear that. At the time, did you make him aware of Dave Clark or not?"

"Not. I was too scared to get involved. It's haunted me for years. Maybe I should have made an anonymous call to the police. I never thought about doing it at the time."

Sally narrowed her eyes as her brain kicked up a gear. "Are you the person who rang me recently?"

"Me? No, why would I have any need to have contacted you?"

"I received an anonymous tip-off, you see, that led to the discovery. I suppose I'm guilty of putting two and two together and coming up with five." Sally's adrenaline was pumping harder and faster around her veins. "Do you believe this man was behind Amanda's kidnapping? Not forgetting her children in all of this, too."

"I've lain awake at night and often thought it over but I'm not one to cast aspersions without having any evidence to hand. There wasn't any of that. Oh God, I feel awful now."

"I don't understand why you wouldn't raise a concern if you and Amanda were that close. What am I missing here, Milly?"

She lowered her head and twisted a pen through her fingers. "Oh God... I genuinely believed she'd run off with him. Thought the kidnap was a setup just to extort the funds from Tim and that she'd run away with this guy to a different country."

"But she was your best friend. Did she mention any of this to you?"

"No, I've always had a vivid imagination, I just presumed it happened that way. I feel terrible now."

"But I repeat, wouldn't your best friend have revealed the truth to you, if that was the plan?"

Milly shrugged and glanced up at Sally. "I feel such an idiot now that she's been found. I'm a romantic at heart. I thought she was off having the time of her life with a new love somewhere."

Sally was floored by the woman's admission. "How often does a mother leave her children behind?"

"God, don't say that. The thought never even occurred to

me. You've got to understand, this place has been super busy over the years, and I've had to dedicate a lot of my spare time thinking about the salon. That sounds a shallow excuse, but it's the truth. I didn't have the headspace to think about both things at once. Her disappearance and my business."

Lorne entered the room and retook her seat. "All actioned." Her gaze shifted between Sally and Milly several times. "What have I missed?"

"I'll fill you in once we're in the car."

"She's annoyed with me," Milly whined.

"You are? Why?" Lorne asked.

Sally's eyes widened, warning Lorne to back off. "Is there any other vital information you neglected to tell Addis at the time that you believe we should know?"

Milly shifted uncomfortably in her seat. "I don't believe so. I have a customer now, so I'm drawing this interview to a close."

"Not so fast, Milly. Yes, we're going to leave now, but I'm also going to need to get a statement from you. When can that be arranged?"

"Ring me later. Here's my card. I have to go."

The three of them left the office. Milly went one way and Sally and Lorne headed back into the salon.

"What's going on?" Lorne whispered.

"I'll tell you in a moment. Leave it for now." Sally's insides were bubbling that much, as soon as they left the salon and turned the corner, she let out a scream.

"What the fuck? You could have warned me you were going to do that. You nearly made me shit myself. What's going on, Sal?"

They made it back to the car before Sally had calmed down enough to tell her. "You drive, and I'll tell you what went on."

"Deal."

Lorne adjusted the driver's seat to suit her shorter legs and started the engine. "Back to the station via the dentist's, right?"

"Yes."

"Come on, I'm dying to hear what's put you in this foul mood."

"People's bloody ignorance, that's what. Can you believe the nerve of that woman? Amanda's so-called best friend."

"You're going to have to give me more than that. When I left you, you were both getting on okay. What changed?"

"Everything. I asked her if Amanda had been having an affair. Initially, she said no, and then she admitted there was some kind of dalliance with Dave Clark, sorry, you know that part. I'm losing my mind here."

"It's okay. What else did she say about this bloke? Apart from him being an ex-con?"

"That she thought Amanda had gone off with him and the whole kidnapping fiasco was a setup to extort funds out of Tim."

"Was she serious?"

"Totally. I asked her if she'd informed Addis at the time. She said no, he didn't appear to be that interested. Jesus wept, what is wrong with people? As coppers, we're only interested if someone tells us something that we would find intriguing. That's how an investigation begins, isn't it?"

"Are you sensing an ulterior motive here?"

"I wouldn't like to say. Then, she goes on to tell me that maybe she should have made an anonymous call to the station."

"What? Do you think she's the one who told you about the house in Acle?"

"I came right out and asked her, thinking it was too much of a coincidence. She flat-out denied it."

"Christ, I can see why you're so incensed. Why hasn't she come forward before this?"

"Because she genuinely believed Amanda had gone off with this fella. I asked her about the kids, and she just shrugged. Then she said the business took up much of her time and she couldn't devote so much thinking time to her friend's plight."

"What utter bollocks that is. We were told the business only got busy *after* the pandemic, not before. That was three years ago. Amanda went missing five years ago. Something isn't adding up here."

"I agree. Do you think she's part of the scam? If it is a scam. God, what a bloody mess, and at the heart of it is a desperate man and his poor kids. They're the ones who have been suffering all these years. I really don't know what to believe. We need to find this Dave Clark and have a chat with him. If his reputation is to be believed, we'll need to take backup with us."

"I'm with you a hundred percent. What are you going to do about Milly?"

"I'm going to run it past the chief, see what he thinks. What a bloody day this has been, and it's not over yet."

Lorne placed a hand on her thigh and squeezed it. "Don't let the fuckers get to you."

"That's going to be bloody hard, they already have."

THEY MANAGED to catch the dentist open on their way and arrived at the station at five forty-five.

"I know it's been a long day, folks, but bear with me for another fifteen minutes, and then we'll call it a day and start over again tomorrow." Sally ran through what each of their visits that afternoon had produced.

Every member of her team seemed shocked by Milly's revelation.

"So, in the morning, we get cracking first thing. I'll be here at seven-thirty if anyone wants to join me, although it's not obligatory in the slightest. I sense we're getting close now. What bothers me is that the clues were there all along, but the previous SIO missed them. Why? How does something like that happen? Is this Warren, the only other officer we've heard mentioned to date, still working at the station?"

Jordan nodded. "Yes, want me to have a word with him?"

"No. I'll request his attendance in my office first thing and go from there. Let's see if he can add anything else to this debacle. What do we know about Addis? What was his cause of death? Anyone know?"

Stuart raised his hand. "I researched it, thinking you'd want to know. His wife, they'd been separated a few months, found him at home with a tub of pills and a bottle of whisky lying beside him. She called an ambulance as he was still alive, but he died on the way to the hospital. Could there be something more sinister in that?"

"You mean, perhaps he was forced to take the concoction?" Sally asked, her brain working overtime.

"Yes, it's not unheard of, the lead investigator being got at like that," Jordan pitched in.

"Let's keep that in mind for a moment and deal with the other shit that's come our way today."

The phone on Joanna's desk rang. She answered it and held it out for Sally. "It's Milly Rowlandson, boss. She wants a word with you."

Sally trotted across the room and took the call. "Milly, is there something else you've remembered?" She tried to keep her tone light and positive, despite her stomach churning itself into knots. She put the phone on speaker and placed a finger to her lips, warning the team to keep quiet.

"I did. I'm sorry I had to dash off and see to my customer."

"No need to apologise. What can you tell me?"

"I swear this is the truth and I haven't made it up."

"Go on."

"Well, the reason Amanda was interested in this Clark fella was because she suspected Tim was having a fling with someone at the factory."

"Does this person have a name?"

"It was a secretary, not his PA, but one of the others who worked there. She was called either Eve or Eva, I believe. I just thought you should know, after me keeping the information quiet about Clark. I'm truly sorry about that."

"It's okay. As they say, the truth always finds its way out into the open sooner or later. We'll do some extra digging. Thank you for letting me know."

"You're welcome. Goodnight, Inspector. Maybe I'll be able to sleep better tonight."

"A clear conscience is good for the soul. Goodnight, Milly." Sally hung up. "Well, well, well. What do you know, she came through in the end. Do we have a list of employees at the factory in the original files?"

Joanna sifted through some paperwork and handed a sheet to Sally. She scanned the list and prodded at a name.

"Bingo, Eva Long. We'll trace her in the morning, then Lorne and I will pay her a visit. Lots on the agenda for tomorrow, peeps. Let's call it a day. You've all worked your socks off today, I'm proud of what we've achieved."

CHAPTER 11

*S*ally drove into work the following day after only getting about two hours' sleep all told. Simon had finally had enough of her tossing and turning and moved into the spare room at around three. He wasn't a happy bunny at the breakfast table. Sally had avoided the expected inquisition concerning her sleepless night by grabbing a croissant and downing a glass of orange juice on her way through the kitchen at seven.

"Have a good day," he shouted after her.

"You, too. Love you."

Dex had sensed the atmosphere and wisely stayed put in his basket in the corner of the kitchen.

"Don't worry, I'll walk Dex this morning," he called out.

She cringed and replied, "You're a gem, thank you."

"Don't forget it," he responded sarcastically.

SHE ENTERED the main office and was shocked to find the rest of the team already hard at it at their desks. "What the...?

You guys must be as insane as me. How did you all sleep last night?"

One by one, they responded that they hadn't had much sleep at all.

"Right, as suspected, this case has worked its way under our skin. So, I say we hit the ground running this morning. Joanna, you man the phones while the rest of us try and tie up the loose ends that are dangling enticingly for us at the moment."

"Yes, boss," Joanna said.

"What we need is to do more house-to-house enquiries, to find out who visited the property in Acle and what connections we can build. Jordan and Stuart, why don't you head over there this morning?"

Jordan looked dubious about the assignment.

"Let's hear it, Jordan, you're obviously not thrilled with that prospect."

"Sorry, boss. I didn't mean to question your authority."

"But?" Sally sensed he wanted to say more.

"Forgive me if I'm speaking out of turn, but… I thought our priority this morning would be finding Dave Clark."

Sally pointed at him. "And you're right. Did any of you manage to find out anything about him yesterday?"

"Not much," Jordan replied. "I got as far as establishing he was in prison for robbery and an assault charge, back in two thousand and seventeen."

"I agree, not much at all. Joanna, why don't you take up the search for him? See if he's got a parole officer. Go down the usual routes of trying to find any vehicles registered to him, electoral roll, whether he has a library card… that was a joke by the way," she added when no one laughed.

"I'll get on it right away," Joanna said.

The main door opened, and a man with fuzzy blond hair

poked his head into the room. "Er... your boss wanted to see me first thing. I'm Warren Hall."

Sally stepped forward and extended her hand. "Pleased to meet you, I'm DI Sally Parker. Come through to my office, we can have a chat in there. No need to look so worried, I've eaten this morning."

"Good to meet you, ma'am." Warren smiled and closed the outer door behind him.

"Lorne, will you join us and bring some coffees with you?"

"Tea for me, nice and strong." Warren grinned.

"Jordan and Stuart, why don't you get on the road early? See if you can catch the homeowners in before they head off to work for the day."

Both men left their seats and tucked the chairs under their desks.

"Come with me, Warren." Sally led the way into her office. "Take a seat, and please, relax, this is just an informal chat."

"With respect, ma'am, that's twice now you've told me not to be worried."

Sally laughed and sat. "Honestly, don't be. I'll start when my partner gets here. What time are you due to begin your shift?"

"At around eight. Can you give me a hint as to what this is about?"

Lorne entered and put three mugs on the desk. "A tea for you, Warren."

He reached for the mug. "Thanks, this'll help set me up for the day."

Lorne closed the door and removed her notebook from her pocket. "Ready when you are," she said, her pen poised.

"Looks ominous," Warren commented.

"Okay, the reason I've asked you to drop by is because we've had to reopen a kidnapping case you were involved with."

Warren inclined his head and frowned. "Not the Amanda Farrant case?"

Sally smiled. "That's correct. We have reason to believe her body has been discovered, although we've yet to receive a formal ID of the remains."

"Remains? Oh my... I always felt sure that she would show up alive somewhere."

"May I ask why you would come to that conclusion?"

He ran a hand around his face as he thought. "I don't know. In my opinion, there was something about the case that didn't quite add up. One of those cases that gnaws away at your gut for no particular reason."

"Funny you should mention that, we said the same last night before the end of our shift. The team agreed that this one was getting under their skin. Tell me this, is that how it was for DI Addis when he was put in charge of the case?"

Warren took a sip from his drink and then shook his head. "I don't think I could ever say that. He ran the investigation... poorly. Again, that's only my opinion."

"Can you tell us why you think that?"

"Hard to put my finger on it. I failed to do it back then as well. He began enthusiastically enough, however, a few days into the investigation something changed."

Sally held her mug up to her mouth and asked, "Care to enlighten us?" Then she took a sip of her coffee and replaced her mug on the desk.

"That's just it, I can't, not really. I was assigned to be with Tim, once he came out of hospital. The poor bloke was absolutely distraught. I often wonder how the family are getting on. I should have stayed in touch with them, but the more time elapsed, the more inclined I was to leave well alone."

"I'm sure Tim would appreciate you dropping by to see him. We visited him yesterday, and he successfully identified two pieces of jewellery which belonged to his wife that were found at the scene. He's beside himself. From what he told us, he's a stay-at-home dad with no job prospects because of him being declared bankrupt. The kids came home from school, and from what we saw, their relationship with their father is somewhat fractious at best."

"That's a shame. He fought long and hard to free them. Last I heard, they'd been found and had returned home to him, but that was months after they'd been kidnapped."

"Tim said they were sold into slavery, so you can imagine the damage that has caused."

"Bloody hell, I hadn't heard about that. I feel guilty about not getting in touch with him now. I thought it would be better to keep my distance once his kids were home, so I didn't act as a constant reminder, showing up at their door. How awful for them all. I hope they received counselling to cope with the emotional baggage."

"One child is still receiving it today, that's the girl, the boy is a different story. I advised Tim he should seek out some counselling as well, especially now his wife's body has been found, or who we presume to be his wife."

"Makes sense. May I ask where the remains were discovered?"

"At a house over in Acle. Can you recall that area being significant during the investigation?"

He paused and took another sip. "No, I don't think it was ever mentioned, not from what I can remember."

"Going back to Addis, were you on duty when the news broke about his death?"

"Yes. To say I was shocked would be an understatement."

"Did he appear suicidal to you?"

"I've not come across anyone who has succeeded in

committing suicide, so I don't feel I have enough experience to answer that question."

"That aside, would you have classed him as either suicidal or depressed?"

"At a push, no, I wouldn't. However, don't people mask how they really feel in public? I'm thinking about Robin Williams here."

"I understand what you're saying. Wasn't Addis separated from his wife at the time?"

"He was and he seemed okay about it. I can't even say the investigation pushed him to his limit. As I've already stated, his enthusiasm in the case waned swiftly, which surprised the hell out of me, considering there were three people's lives at risk. In truth, it frustrated me no end, and I know Tim was affected by Addis' crummy attitude as well."

"Hmm… is there any chance he was involved with the gang?"

Warren snorted. "You tell me. He was a very complex man, didn't really open up to anyone, not from what I could tell."

"Okay, some of the witnesses we've spoken to have told us that he asked very few questions during the investigation. Was that your experience?"

"Hard to say. My principal role was babysitting Tim, therefore, I spent most of my time at his mansion instead of with the rest of the team at the station. I was kept out of the loop, don't ask me why."

"Did you get the impression that Tim was having an affair?"

Warren laughed. "Not at all. He didn't sneak off to make secret phone calls, he was happy to deal with anyone who rang in front of me, kidnappers and family alike. There was no hint of him speaking to anyone discreetly. Poor bloke was desperate to get his family back. He lost everything because of those damn kidnappers."

"We know. I suspect he's a shadow of his former self today. Last question, then I'll let you get on with your day. Who made the call for you to leave Tim?"

"It was only supposed to be a temporary arrangement for a couple of days. Addis withdrew me from the house once the kidnappers told Tim they wouldn't be contacting him again. That was after the ten mill was paid."

"I see. Okay, thanks for speaking with me today. If anything else crops up, would it be all right if I give you a call?"

He finished off his drink, wiped his mouth on the sleeve of his jacket and stood. "Sure thing. Feel free to contact me if you need to know anything else, ma'am. I wish you well with the investigation. It's going to be hard tracking down the people responsible, over five years later."

"Agreed. Speak soon, possibly."

He left the room, and Sally glanced out of the window at the dark clouds effortlessly floating past.

"Not sure if speaking to Warren has muddied the waters or not. Even he's under the impression that something didn't add up at the time. But, I'm not going to sit here dwelling on it, we have work to do."

"Are we going to pay the secretary a visit?" Lorne asked.

"If we can track her down, yes."

They finished their drinks and joined Joanna in the office.

"How's it going?" Sally perched on the desk next to Joanna's.

"I've got an address for Dave Clark, and I think I've got one for Eva Long. I'm double-checking that before I come to you with a definitive answer."

"That's great news, Joanna. You're brilliant. I'm regretting sending the boys off to carry out the house-to-house enquiries now."

"A couple of hours isn't going to make any difference," Lorne said. "You could always ask a patrol car to keep an eye on Clark, from a distance."

"You think? The last thing we want to do is scare him off. Why don't we head over to have a word with Eva and see how that pans out? Hopefully the boys will be back after lunch, and we can go in force to pay Clark a visit, then."

"Sounds like a plan to me."

Sally picked up the sheet with both addresses written on it and gave Joanna the thumbs-up. "Keep digging for us. Also, can you see if Lester Farrant is on our radar yet? Word has it that he's been hanging out with a gang. I'd like to steady that ship before it starts listing, causing Tim even more problems to have to cope with."

"Leave it with me, I'll see what I can find out."

SALLY KNOCKED on the door of the detached house on one of the older estates, only for it to remain unanswered. "I wonder where she works. Let's see if the neighbours know. You take that side."

They separated, and it was Lorne who came up trumps with the answer. "At the sports club in Hethersett, so not too far away."

"Okay, back to the car we go."

They were ten minutes away from their destination when Sally's mobile rang.

"Can you get that? At a glance, I think it's Jordan's number."

"Hi, Jordan, it's Lorne. I'm putting you on speaker."

"Hi. We've got some news."

"Go on," Sally prompted. She searched up ahead for a lay-by to pull into. There wasn't one, not on this stretch of the B1172.

"We took a punt and asked at the local newsagent's on the estate. The shop owner has been there for thirty years and said she knew everyone's business, in a nice way, of course."

"And?" Sally asked.

"And, she told us that a young lady used to pay Nancy Hart's paper bill for her."

"Interesting, and did this young lady have a name?"

"She did. Eva."

Sally swiftly cast a glance in Lorne's direction and then back at the road. "Crap, okay. We're ten minutes or there-abouts away from her place of work. We'll bring her in for questioning as you've uncovered a connection to the crime scene. Well done to both of you. See you back at the station. No, wait, Lorne will give you Dave Clark's address. A patrol car is on its way, but I'm concerned they'll be seen. I want you to head over there and relieve them. Keep in touch."

"Will do, boss."

Lorne ended the call. "Sounds like it's all coming together now."

"Yes, piece by piece. Let's hope it doesn't backfire on us."

"Keep positive."

ONCE THEY ARRIVED, the receptionist rang Eva and asked her to come to the main entrance. The blonde woman in her early thirties eyed Sally and Lorne with concern as she walked down the corridor towards them.

Sally produced her ID. "Eva Long? I'm DI Sally Parker, and this is my partner, DS Lorne Warner. We'd like a word with you down at the station."

"Are you forcing me to come with you?"

"If you want to put it that way, yes. Or you have the option to come willingly, which will go more in your favour. The choice is yours."

"Can I get my bag?"

"Yes. You have five minutes."

Eva set off up the narrow hallway to one of the rooms at the end. She was gone longer than either of them anticipated.

Sally approached the receptionist and asked, "Is there a way out of the building back there?"

"No, there's not."

With that, an alarm sounded.

"Shit, yes there is, the emergency exit. Go to the end, up one flight of stairs, and you'll see the door on the right. Excuse me, I need to try and turn it off."

"I'll try and head her off," Lorne said and darted out of the front door.

Leaving Sally to bolt down the length of the corridor, wishing she'd chosen to wear a flatter pair of shoes. She climbed the stairs and pushed open the fire escape that was ajar, only to see Lorne tackling Eva to the ground on the grassy bank close to the car park.

Her partner had slapped the cuffs on her by the time an out-of-breath Sally got there.

"Have you read her rights to her?"

"I have. She spat at me in response."

"How uncouth. On your feet, Eva, we've got a few questions we need to ask you back at the station."

"You're wasting your time, I'll be going down the 'no comment' route."

"We'll see about that," Lorne said.

Between them, they managed to haul Eva to her feet and marched her towards their vehicle.

Once the suspect was placed in the back seat, Sally said over the roof of the car, "I'm going to enjoy this particular battle."

"Let's hope she changes her mind during the drive."

CHAPTER 12

They booked Eva in with the Custody Sergeant and went upstairs until the duty solicitor could attend the interview. In the meantime, Jordan and Stuart were on the tail of Dave Clark who had left his swanky detached home on the outskirts of town and was driving his Tesla through the narrow back lanes towards Norwich.

"Is he on to you?" Sally asked.

"Not sure," Jordan replied. "We're keeping our distance. Oops, I spoke too soon. He's put his foot down."

"Stick with him. Use your siren, and let control know your location. I'll make sure the area is flooded with patrol cars. Don't let him out of your sight, he's running for a reason. I'll get a warrant organised for his address."

"Rightio, boss. We'll be in touch soon."

"Good luck, but more importantly, stay safe."

Sally hung up and covered her face with her hands and groaned. "I reckon he's got wind of us picking up Eva, but how? There has to be a connection between them."

"I'd say you've hit the nail on the head with that conclusion," Lorne said. "Want me to organise a warrant?"

"Please."

Pat, the desk sergeant on duty, rang Sally not long after, informing her that the solicitor had arrived and that he'd taken her to Interview Room Two to allow her to have a word with her client.

Sally and Lorne descended the stairs and entered the interview room to find Eva having a chat with the female solicitor. The woman was unknown to Sally.

She offered her hand. "DI Sally Parker."

"I'm relatively new. Tania Bryant. Pleased to meet you, Inspector. I've had a brief chat with my client. She's totally dumbfounded about why you've dragged her in here today."

"Let's make a start and all will be revealed. One question, if I may? If your client is innocent, then why did she run from us?"

Bryant faced her client. Eva kept her head bowed and mumbled an apology.

"I wasn't aware of that fact. Thank you for filling me in." Bryant smiled and rolled her eyes while her client was distracted.

"My pleasure. Sergeant, if you can get the interview underway."

Lorne said the necessary for the recording, and Sally asked her first question.

"Eva Long, how do you know Tim Farrant?"

"I worked at his factory."

"Rumour has it that you were having an affair with him, is that correct?"

"No comment."

Sally went on to ask several more questions about Eva's previous employment and received the same answer. Then she decided to change tack. "What's your connection to Nancy Hart?"

That got Eva's attention. She shot Sally a look through narrowed eyes. "What?"

"Come now, I'm sure you heard the question just fine. What's your connection with the old woman?"

Eva gulped, and her head lowered again. She whispered her response, "She was my mother's dear friend."

"Ah, okay. And how do you know Dave Clark?"

Again, her head shot up, and her gaze bore into Sally's.

"I don't."

"Credit us with some sense, Eva. While the investigation might be new to us, there are a lot of facts, loose ends if you will, that have been left dangling for over five years. What was your part in the kidnapping of Amanda Farrant, Tim's wife?"

"No comment."

"It doesn't take a genius to figure out there's a connection, not when you were having an affair with her husband. In the way, was she? Did you come up with the kidnapping plan? Did Tim have anything to do with it? No, wait, we've got information that Dave Clark was seeing Amanda. Did they come up with the idea of holding her and her children hostage? What went wrong? Or did it?"

"I… no, I'm not going there. No comment."

"What proof do you have apart from hearsay, Inspector?" Bryant demanded.

"I'm coming to that. There was lots of evidence that the previous officer in charge of the case chose to ignore, or did he? Was he part of this audacious plan? Twenty million would have set you all up for life, wouldn't it? Addis included. What went wrong? Why did you kill Addis?"

"I didn't. I had nothing to do with that. I swear I didn't. Please, you have to help me. If they find out I'm here, they'll kill me."

"They? Give us the names of all the people involved in

this kidnapping plot, and I'll see if I can get you a deal with the Crown Prosecution Service. On the other hand, if you choose to keep your mouth shut, you'll all spend a long time behind bars for the kidnapping and murder of Amanda Farrant. The choice is yours."

"I didn't kill her. I tried to do everything I could to help her but..."

Sally's eyes narrowed. "You're the one who rang me, who told me where to find her remains, aren't you?"

"Yes, I couldn't live with the guilt any longer, or her screams haunting my dreams any more."

"Thank you for finally doing the right thing. Have you seen Tim lately?"

"No, I cut all ties with him once Amanda was kidnapped. In truth, he was the one who pushed me aside. He told me he needed to concentrate on getting his wife back. Told me he didn't realise how much he loved her until she went missing."

"And the kids, of course."

"Yes, them, too."

"I repeat, how do you know Dave Clark?" Sally asked.

"He's my brother's best friend, or he was at the time. It was Mike's idea for Dave to get friendly with Amanda, so it would be easy to abduct her."

"Why put her kids through that ordeal? Whose idea was it to involve them?"

"Mike, my brother. He thought it would give us more leverage to take the kids as well."

"And when Tim failed to come up with the full amount, whose idea was it to put the kids into slavery?"

"That was Dave's. He's a cruel bastard. He constantly raped Amanda in front of her kids. You have to believe me, things went far too far for me. I didn't sign up for that type of shit."

"Did you try and prevent any of it from happening?"

"Like I said, Dave's a cruel bastard. There are some people in this world you know not to tackle."

"If you thought that, then why the hell did you get involved with him in the first place?"

"My brother blackmailed me into working with them. He said he would tell Amanda the truth about Tim and me if I didn't do as they said."

"And things escalated from there? Is that what you're telling me? They got greedy, always wanting more?"

"Yes. Hence the kids being sold into slavery. Tim was lucky he got them back. I've heard of kids being transferred to another country and dying at the hands of their 'new owners'. I couldn't bear to think of the kids going through that."

"And yet it took you five years to come forward, and then, only after you'd fallen out with your brother? I find that extremely hard to comprehend."

A knock on the door interrupted the interview, and Joanna entered the room and asked to have a quiet word with Sally in the hallway. Sally excused herself from the interview for the recording and left the room.

"I thought you should know ASAP. The Tesla crashed and…"

"No, don't tell me Clark is dead?" Sally asked, shocked by the news.

"He's in a bad way en route to hospital."

"That's something. Okay, I'd better get back in there and complete the interview while she's in a talkative mood. While you're here, I need you to also look into someone else's background for me."

"Who's that?"

She thumbed over her shoulder at the interview room. "Her brother, Mike Long. He's Clark's best friend. I'll go over the details later, once I've finished with her. Also, dig into their social media accounts. We're still missing the names of the other gang members."

"I'll see what I can find."

"Thanks, Joanna." Sally entered the interview room again and jotted down the information for Lorne to read.

Her partner raised an eyebrow but said nothing.

"Is there something we should know, Inspector?" Bryant probed.

"Actually, I don't see any harm in telling your client the news that Clark is now in hospital. Fighting for his life after crashing his car in a high-speed chase with members of my team."

"Good. I hope he doesn't make it," Eva mumbled and rubbed her hands.

"That's not nice," Bryant said.

"I've already told you he's a cruel bastard. If you knew him like I do, you'd be sitting here saying the same."

Sally cleared her throat to get the interview back on track. "Going back to the other members of the group, are you prepared to give us their names? The net is closing in on all of you, it would be a shame if only three of you went down for the crimes and the others got let off scot-free."

She shrugged. "I don't know. You'll have to ask either Dave or Mike, I'm sure they'll be eager to come to some sort of deal with you."

"It ain't gonna happen. I don't do deals with killers."

"Then you're going to have to find them the old-fashioned way."

"Don't worry, we're already on the case. Is there anything else you want to add?"

"No. I'm tired and need a rest."

"It can be utterly exhausting, unburdening yourself of the truth. I want to thank you for finally having the courage to do the right thing." Sally gestured for Lorne to conclude the interview.

The female officer at the rear of the room stepped forward and tapped Eva on the shoulder. "I'll take you back to your cell, Miss Long."

Sally accompanied Ms Bryant to the exit and thanked her for attending so promptly.

"My pleasure. I admire your interviewing technique, Inspector, it was spot-on. I should imagine you got to the truth in record time."

Sally felt like breathing on her nails and rubbing her fingers on her chest, but she refrained from coming across as a smug cow.

EPILOGUE

"*A*re we ready for the off?" Sally asked Simon, Lorne and Tony. She ruffled Dex's head. He was just as excited as they were. He loved it aboard her father's boat.

"I'm really looking forward to it. It's a shame your mum and dad aren't well enough to join us," Lorne said.

"It is, but I have a surprise waiting for you down at the dock." Sally winked and put the last bag of goodies into the boot of their car.

"Of course there's no point in me asking you what you're on about, is there?"

"Nope, you'll find out soon enough."

The journey got underway. It was only a fifteen-minute ride to the boatyard where her father moored his cruiser. Simon drove while Lorne and Tony followed in their car.

"I wonder if she's here yet," Sally asked.

"From what I can remember, she's always been punctual in the past. Lorne is going to get the shock of her life."

"Good. That sounded heartless, didn't it?"

They laughed.

Another right turn, and they drew into the boatyard.

There was no sign of their surprise guest yet. Sally's heart sank. She checked her mobile. She had no new messages, so she presumed everything was still okay.

The four of them unloaded the cars, then Simon got ready to cast off. It was then that Sally noticed a car pull into the boatyard. She distracted Lorne, asked her if she would give her an opinion on something below deck.

"Sure, but can't it wait? I love this part of the trip."

"Not really. You think I'd be asking if it could?"

"All right, there's no need to get snotty with me."

Sally caught Lorne rolling her eyes at her husband behind her back in one of the mirrors on deck and sniggered. The men were in on the surprise. It had taken a lot to organise and had nearly fallen through at the last minute.

"What's so important that I have to leave my post for?" Lorne enquired, her brow furrowed into a deep frown.

"I was wondering what dress to wear for tonight's meal. The red or the blue?"

"Is this some kind of joke? Since when do you ask for fashion advice from me? Bloody hell, Sal. Either of them, you'll look stunning in both. There, decision made. I'm going back up on deck now."

"Wait, what about shoes? The black or blue ones?"

"Christ. Black if you choose the red, and blue with the blue, or mix and match. It doesn't matter, it'll all work out fine."

Lorne went on ahead of her a few steps before Sally called out, "Wait, what colour handbag should I take?"

Lorne turned back and tutted. "White or black. Who cares? We're going for a pub meal, not tea at the bloody Ritz."

"What are you wearing?"

Lorne held her arms out to the sides and said, "What you see is what you get. Is that it? Can we go now?"

Sally nodded and squeezed past her partner to ensure she reached the deck first.

"How rude," Lorne complained under her breath.

"It's knowing your status in life," Sally shot back at her.

"Bloody charming."

On deck, Sally could see the surprise guest had arrived and was sitting at the back, near the wheelhouse where Simon and Tony were standing, shielding her from view.

"I never thought I'd ever hear you say that," Lorne added, still moaning.

"Stop your whinging and fix us a drink. I'll have a glass of what our guest is having." Sally stood to the side.

Lorne's gaze was drawn to the mystery newcomer. She screamed and ran past Sally into her daughter's arms. "Charlie, what the heck are you doing here? Not that I'm complaining."

"Sally asked me to join you all for the weekend."

They hugged, and then Lorne stepped forward and hugged Sally tightly. "Thank you, I needed this after all the memories this case has stirred up this week."

"I know you did."

As the boys cast off and the boat chugged along, Charlie wanted to know the ins and outs of the latest case they'd solved.

Between them, Sally and Lorne filled her in.

"Crap, that poor man and his children, they'll be emotionally scarred for life now," Charlie said.

Lorne frowned. "What, like you were? Kids can be more resilient than adults give them credit for."

Charlie sighed. "All right, smarty-pants. Will he get his money back?"

Sally nodded. "What's left of it. We've got all the members of the gang in custody now, awaiting trial. I've filed a report requesting Tim's money is returned to him under The

Proceeds of Crime Act. I'll give him all the help he needs to rebuild his life and to be able to give his children the future they deserve. The gang's assets will be seized next week."

"What about this Clark fella? What injuries has he sustained?"

"Nothing major, not really. A few broken bones in one of his legs and a collapsed lung. It could have been so much worse. He's on the mend. I suppose he's thinking you can't keep a good man down, but we'll ensure he spends the rest of his life behind bars, exactly where he belongs. Anyway, enough about work, we're here to have a good time. So let's raise our glasses. To Charlie, thank you for joining us on this adventure. Let's hope it's the first of many."

It will be if I have my way.

THE END

THANK you for reading The Good Die Young. The next book in this exciting cold case series **Coping Without You** is now available.

IN THE MEANTIME, have you read any of my other fast paced crime thrillers yet? Why not try the first book in the DI Sara Ramsey series No Right to Kill

OR GRAB the first book in the bestselling, award-winning, Justice series here, Cruel Justice.

. . .

OR THE FIRST book in the spin-off Justice Again series, Gone In Seconds.

WHY NOT TRY the first book in the DI Sam Cobbs series, set in the beautiful Lake District, To Die For.

PERHAPS YOU'D PREFER to try one of my other police procedural series, the DI Kayli Bright series which begins with The Missing Children.

OR MAYBE YOU'D enjoy the DI Sally Parker series set in Norfolk, Wrong Place.

OR MY GRITTY police procedural starring DI Nelson set in Manchester, Torn Apart.

OR MAYBE YOU'D like to try one of my successful psychological thrillers She's Gone, I KNOW THE TRUTH or Shattered Lives.

KEEP IN TOUCH WITH M A COMLEY

Pick up a FREE novella by signing up to my newsletter today.
https://BookHip.com/WBRTGW

BookBub
www.bookbub.com/authors/m-a-comley

Blog

http://melcomley.blogspot.com

Why not join my special Facebook group to take part in monthly giveaways.

Readers' Group

Printed in Great Britain
by Amazon

40417181R00126